THE
BILLION DOLLAR RANSOM

THE HARDY BOYS ® MYSTERY STORIES

THE
BILLION DOLLAR
RANSOM

Franklin W. Dixon

Illustrated by Leslie Morrill

WANDERER BOOKS

Published by Simon & Schuster, New York

Copyright © 1982 by Stratemeyer Syndicate
Published by WANDERER BOOKS
A Simon & Schuster Division of
Gulf & Western Corporation
Simon & Schuster Building
1230 Avenue of the Americas
New York, New York 10020

Manufactured in the United States of America
10 9 8 7 6 5 4 3 2

THE HARDY BOYS is a trademark of Stratemeyer Syndicate,
registered in the United States Patent and Trademark Office

WANDERER and colophon are trademarks of Simon & Schuster

Library of Congress Cataloging in Publication Data

Dixon, Franklin W.
The billion dollar ransom.

(The Hardy boys mystery stories ; 73)
Summary: The Hardy boys help out when a magicians'
tournament is threatened by mysterious happenings.
[1. Mystery and detective stories. 2. Magic trick—Fiction]
I. Morrill, Leslie H., ill. II. Title. III. Series:
Dixon, Franklin W. Hardy boys mystery stories ; 73.
PZ7.D644Bi   [Fic]   81–16112
ISBN 0–671–42352–5   AACR2
ISBN 0–671–42355–X (pbk.)

Contents

1 Tournament of Magic

". . . and so I'm afraid that the show will end in disaster!" Mr. Heifitz concluded.

"Let me get this straight, Mr. Heifitz," Fenton Hardy, the famous detective, said while glancing at his two sons at the other side of the study. "You are going to put on a tournament of magicians that is to decide who is the best in the country. This will take place over a period of four days starting tomorrow night, and half of the magicians will be eliminated after each show—"

"Eliminated by the three expert judges," the manager and owner of the Bayport Palace Theater interrupted.

"By three expert judges. The tournament was

originally scheduled for a Boston theater that unfortunately was destroyed by a fire."

"By a *mysterious* fire that is suspected to be arson."

"And you want us to handle the security during the performances," Mr. Hardy said.

"Yes, yes," Mr. Heifitz said eagerly.

There was a long silence in the study as Mr. Hardy looked out the window on a beautiful summer afternoon. Frank and Joe, sitting on the large leather couch, believed their father was trying to think of a polite refusal. They were surprised when his gaze finally returned to Mr. Heifitz and he said, "We'll do it."

The elderly white-haired man jumped to his feet and grasped the detective's hand enthusiastically. "Thank you, Fenton, thank you! I knew you wouldn't let me down."

Mr. Hardy and his sons accompanied Mr. Heifitz downstairs. "Tell me, though," the detective said at the front door, "why do you believe security is required at the show? Your sense of trouble must be based on more than the Boston fire."

"I must confess that it is. This tournament was arranged by Zandro the Great or, I should say, by Happy Hortell, his manager. Now, Zandro does not have what you'd call an easy personality. You might even say that he seems to go out of his way to earn disfavor by his fellow illusionists. He is decidedly the favorite to win, which will make him hated even more. There will be great tension during the five days, Fenton. I fear that it might result in some sort of violent action."

"If that is so," Mr. Hardy said, "then why did you book the show?"

Mr. Heifitz looked shocked. "And let one of the great events of the century slip right through my fingers? Never! Well, good-bye and thanks once more."

Mr. Hardy watched with amusement as the small man walked jauntily to his car. "Just like his father," he said. "Now there was a showman. One of the best comedians in the East."

He and the boys walked back upstairs to the study. As soon as they were seated, he grinned at his sons. "I can read your thoughts. Why is he taking such an insignificant job, you are saying to yourselves."

"It did cross my mind, Dad," Frank admitted.

"I wouldn't take this assignment for anyone else, but there is a debt of gratitude to be paid," the detective explained. "You know my family didn't have much money when I was going to college. I had a scholarship, but I still had additional expenses and, besides, I wanted to help your grandparents make ends meet. There weren't many jobs around town in those days, but Otto Heifitz—Mr. Heifitz's father—let me be an usher on weekends. He knew my predicament and I believe he overpaid me. His son Jon, who was cashier, was also very kind to me. So if Jon's worried, then it's up to me to help, although I think our greatest problems will be runaway rabbits or lost pigeons."

He was interrupted by the strident ring of his business phone. He picked up the receiver. "Fenton Hardy. Oh, Vito. How are you? It's been, let's see, seven or eight months now since we got together. How's everything in Washington. Today? That's rather short notice, but I can make it to your office in about three hours. You'll meet me at Andrews Air Force Base? This must be pretty serious. I'm on my way."

He replaced the phone and rose. Striding towards the door, he called over his shoulder, "Frank, pull the car around to the front, will you? And, Joe, phone Jack Wayne, please. He's out at the airport today, going over the plane. Tell him to fuel up for a flight to Washington. I'll tell your mother that I'm off for a few hours."

Within five minutes, the three were driving towards Bayport Airport. "Any idea when you'll be home, Dad?" Joe asked.

"Vito said that I should be back tonight," his father said. The boys knew better than to ask who this mysterious Vito was. If Mr. Hardy had wanted them to know, he would have told them. "In the meantime, suppose you go over to the Palace Theater. It would be wise to get an idea of the layout before the tournament opens tomorrow night."

Skyhappy Sal's engines were humming by the time they reached the airport. Jack Wayne waved at them from the pilot's seat. Mr. Hardy wasted no time in boarding the plane, and presently it was cleared for takeoff. Joe and Frank watched it roar down the runway and rise majestically into the sky.

"I wish we were going along, instead of to the Palace to play nursemaid," Joe said wistfully, looking at the aircraft.

Frank started their bright yellow sports sedan and headed back towards the city. "Remember what Dad always says," he remarked. "No case is small if we do our job well."

"Come on, Frank," his younger brother said. "Don't tell me you wouldn't rather be going to Washington."

Frank grinned. "I sure would."

On the marquee of the Palace Theater was the message, MAGICIAN TOURNAMENT FOR THE CHAMPIONSHIP OF THE WORLD WED–SAT. The posters on either side of the doors proclaimed, THE 16 BEST MAGICIANS BATTLE FOR THE WORLD TITLE. DON'T MISS IT! STARRING ZANDRO THE GREAT!

As the Hardys walked into the foyer, they saw

11

Mr. Heifitz backed against the wall by a very angry man. "Why did you let him do that, Heifitz? Why did you let Zandro plaster his name all over the posters? Don't the rest of us count? Don't *I*, Manuel the Magnificent, count?"

"I . . . I . . ." Mr. Heifitz stammered. "I didn't know. Hortell said they would buy the posters and save me money."

"Didn't you realize that egotistical maniac would give himself top billing without mentioning anyone else?" the magician shouted, his voice betraying an Hispanic accent.

"Why don't you take this matter up with Zandro or Hortell?" the theater manager asked placatingly. "I'm sure they would listen to reason."

"Reason! They don't know the meaning of the word!" the other man raged. "I just met Zandro a few minutes ago. We have been enemies for years, but I was willing to forgive and forget. I held out my hand in friendship and told him that I would not try to show him up too badly in the tournament. He had the nerve to scoff at my act of charity and walk by with his nose in the air. I shall destroy him yet! You shall see! There is not enough room in this world for the two of us!"

Manuel then turned on his heel and entered the theater, leaving a nervous Mr. Heifitz behind. The boys walked up to the manager.

12

"He seems very upset, Mr. Heifitz," Frank said.

The theater manager was startled by the boys. "Yes, Manuel is a trifle agitated, but he'll get over it." He shook his head. "Show people are apt to be temperamental, and I must admit that magicians seem to lead all others in this trait. Now what can I do for you two?"

"Our father sent us to look over the theater," Joe answered.

Mr. Heifitz waved towards the doors. "Wander around as much as you like. You must forgive me if I can't give you a guided tour, but I have to go to the printer's to pick up the tickets. Perhaps you'll have the pleasure of meeting Zandro."

"That's a pleasure I'd rather skip," Joe said to Frank as they went into the theater.

"Me, too," Frank said. "Also, that Manuel sounded dangerous to me with his threat to destroy Zandro."

"Did I hear my name?" boomed a jovial voice. A huge man wearing a wide black cape appeared on stage from the wings. "You are a little early for the show. Come tomorrow night to see Zandro in action. I promise you the experience of your young lives."

"We haven't come for the show, Mr. Zandro," Joe informed him. "I'm Joe Hardy and this is my brother Frank."

13

The magician's smile split his round large face. "The Hardys! Heifitz said that he had hired you for security—a very wise move, considering that madman Manuel is on the premises. But where is your father? I have read so much about him and admired him for years. I would dearly like to meet him, one master of his craft greeting another."

"He's busy at the moment," Frank said. "But I'm sure he'll be here during the tournament. We came to look over the theater. We want to know where the exits and dressing rooms are, things like that, which would be difficult to do when all the magicians are here."

"Then let me accompany you," Zandro said. "I played the Palace two years ago and I know something of its design."

The boys stared at each other. The last thing they expected was for Zandro to be friendly and helpful.

The illusionist led them down a backstage hall. "To your right and left are the dressing rooms," he said. "Would you like to see each one?"

"Well, we'd like to see their windows and what lies outside them," Joe said.

"There are no windows on the right, but each room on the left has a window that faces an alley." As he went along, Zandro flung open the doors. "And here at the end is my dressing room." He marched through a door marked by a huge gold star.

A man bending over an open trunk jumped when they entered. "Zandro!" he exclaimed. "I thought you were going out."

"That I was, Happy, but on the way I met these two young men. You are in the presence of fame, my friend. Let me introduce you to Frank and Joe Hardy. Gentlemen, this is Happy Hortell, my manager."

"The sons of Fenton Hardy? Well, this is indeed an honor," the man said, holding out his hand, smiling. He might have passed for a circus tall man, standing almost seven feet high. He was as thin as a rail, and his face resembled a clown's.

Frank and Joe shook hands vigorously with Happy. "I was putting away your equipment," Hortell said, pointing at the trunk.

"We won't disturb you then," Zandro said. "You continue while I show these boys around the place."

In ten minutes, they had taken a tour of the entire theater. "I guess that will do it," Frank said. "Thank you, Mr. Zandro. We've probably held you up from important business."

The magician laughed. "My important business is a trip to nostalgia land. Do you know the old opera house?"

"Sure," Joe said. "It's four blocks from here. It's been closed for years and was going to be torn down for an office building, but a lot of people protested. Now it's been designated as an historical landmark

15

building and is being restored. The Community Arts Association will be using it for plays and concerts. The Prito Construction Company is working on it now."

"I can see that there is little that happens in Bayport that escapes your attention," Zandro remarked. "I was on my way there when I met you. You see, it has a special place in my heart. I did my first show there more than thirty years ago. Would you care to accompany me?"

Frank looked at Joe, who nodded. "We haven't much on our schedule this afternoon. We'd be happy to go."

They walked along Ocean Avenue, enjoying the bright summer sun.

"Are you looking forward to the tournament, Mr. Zandro?" Joe asked.

The magician's face brightened. "Just Zandro, please, not Mr. Zandro. I left my surname in the distant past. Yes, indeed, I am looking forward to this contest. It was my idea, you know. It was to be held in Boston, but an unfortunate fire destroyed the theater. I was in despair until I thought of Bayport and the Palace Theater. What better town in which to be crowned as king of all magicians than the place where I started my career!"

"You're that sure of winning, then?" Frank asked.

"Oh, I shall triumph, never doubt it. There is no

16

one equal to me. But it shall be fun, nevertheless, and marvelous entertainment. Anyway, I suggested Bayport to Happy Hortell and he acted on it immediately. A wonderful manager. He was a magician once, but not very talented, I'm afraid. He befriended me as I was just getting started. When I ran across him years later, he was down on his luck so I offered him a job. I have never regretted it. He's not only an acute businessman, but a good friend as well."

In front of the opera house, Mr. Prito and his son Tony were examining a set of blueprints. The Hardys introduced Zandro, who asked permission to tour the decrepit building.

Mr. Prito scratched his chin. "I don't know. It can be dangerous in there. There are rotten floorboards and the walls are not too safe."

"We promise to be very careful," Zandro said.

"Okay, but stay in the lighted areas," the contractor advised. "You won't find many of those, since a good deal of the electrical system has rotted away."

As the Hardys and Zandro were approaching the main door, two carpenters came out holding a screaming and kicking elderly man.

"You have no right!" the captive yelled, tears of humiliation pouring down his cheeks. I am Jonathan Ridoux, do you hear? Jonathan Ridoux! You dolts, I own the opera house!"

2 *The Ghost in the Dressing Room*

Mr. Prito walked towards Ridoux with his hand raised in a placating manner. "Now, Jonathan," he said, "we all know you have acted here and—"

"Many's the time I have stood bowing at the footlights while the audience rose as if it were one person to cheer and applaud until the stage manager had to ask for silence," the elderly man said, fixing Mr. Prito with a wild look. "The noise was deafening."

"I'm sure you were a great hit. What I don't understand is why you're so against the opera house being restored as it was when you were a star."

"This work must be stopped immediately!" Ridoux screamed. "*They* don't like it and *they* gave me the theater!"

18

"Who doesn't like it?" Mr. Prito asked, puzzled.

The answer came in a half-croak, half-whisper. "The ghosts!" Ridoux gestured aimlessly towards the theater. "The ghosts of the great stars who once stood on the boards in this magnificent structure. People like Lillie Langtry, Joe Jefferson, John Barrymore, Sarah Bernhardt, all the great ones. They have told me it is my duty to prevent your work."

"Mr. Ridoux, if you attempt to break in here once more while the restoration is going on, I shall have to have you arrested," Mr. Prito said gently, but firmly. "You have disturbed us too many times as it is."

"Your threats mean nothing to me," the eccentric old man snarled, breaking away from the man holding him and brushing off his worn and old-fashioned suit. "This devil's labor must be stopped . . . and it will!" He stumbled down the street, muttering to himself.

Mr. Prito shook his head. "Poor old guy. He's kind of a local character. A little off in his head, but he's harmless, I guess. Just gets in the way."

"Oh, I remember him, all right," Zandro said. "No one who played the opera house could forget Jonathan Ridoux, but I never dreamed he was still alive and quite agile, considering his age. He is both comic and tragic. He was born, I understand, into a well-to-do Bayport family. However, he contracted a fatal disease when he was little more than a child."

19

"A fatal disease?" Joe repeated. "But he's still living."

"It's not a disease of the body," Zandro said, "but of the spirit. He fell in love with the stage, and that's an ailment few ever get over. It's all right when one has talent like mine, but it's quite a different story when ability is lacking, as in the case of our unfortunate Ridoux."

"Couldn't act, eh?" Tony Prito asked.

The magician chuckled. "I have seen him try. It was a wretched performance obvious to all but him. I create wonderful illusions, but I could never approach the one he possesses—he thinks he is the greatest actor who ever lived. At any rate, it might have been different had his parents lived." Zandro paused, then went on. "But they passed on when he was twenty. He let the family fortune deteriorate while he pursued his dream. Impressed by his tenacity, several producers gave him tryouts. Yet he would never face reality. He hung around the opera house, waiting for his big chance. The owners gave him odd jobs, which made him quite happy, I believe. But enough of that. Now on to my journey into the land of nostalgia."

He led the way into the theater, followed by Frank and Joe. He paused in the middle of the center aisle. The seats were rotted; some of them

20

had crumbled. Gaudy scenes on the wall were faded, and there were holes showing dirty plaster. "*Sic transit gloria*," the magician said. "So passes glory. But I hear cheerful sounds." From behind the stage came the noise of hammers and electric saws. "This grand old theater will have a rebirth."

He went up to the stage, made a mock bow to an invisible audience, then they all walked out to the wings, past startled workmen, and upstairs to a balcony.

"I was afraid that the dressing room area would be dark," Zandro said to Joe and Frank, "but I see we're in luck." He flung open a door. "Here it is—my first dressing room!"

There was a layer of thick dust everywhere. A makeup table missing two legs lay on the floor. The only further furniture was a chair with no seat.

"It doesn't look like much now and it didn't look like much thirty years ago," Zandro said, "but to me, a young man in his first show, it was a temple. How many before me must have felt the same!" He gnawed his lip for a moment. "You know, Ridoux may have been right about ghosts. I've never been sure. Was I dreaming or did it really happen?"

"Did what happen?" Frank asked.

"Was Alebert Cavendish really in this room?" Zandro asked in a vacant voice.

"Alebert Cavendish?" Frank was beginning to think that Zandro was as nutty as Jonathan Ridoux.

"It was my last night here. I was alone, putting on makeup and concentrating on my act. Suddenly, I saw a tall man in Shakespearean clothes in the mirror. He was glaring at me. If you could only have seen the rage and hate on his face!"

Zandro shuddered. "I have never forgotten it. I whirled around and saw—" His voice dropped to a deep whisper. "Nothing! I searched the room, the closet, the hall. No one! I ran downstairs and out to the box office where I told the theater manager about it. He laughed and told me not to worry, that I had only seen the harmless ghost of Alebert Cavendish."

Zandro shook himself out of his half-trance and looked at the boys' concerned faces. "He said that this Cavendish, an Englishman, had been playing the ghost of Hamlet's father in 1902. My dressing room had been his. He was coming down the stairs when he tripped and broke his neck. His ghost had apparently appeared in this room several times since."

The magician laughed. "You look skeptical, and I don't blame you. I was in an excited state that night due to my first success, and my imagination was possibly over-stimulated. Nevertheless, I always insisted on having another dressing room whenever I played here."

"And you never saw the ghost again?" Joe asked.

"Never, and I hope I never shall!" the magician said vehemently. "But that's enough about spirits. It's too nice a day to be morbid. Anyway, I'm going back to the Palace."

"We should, too," Frank said. "We left our car there."

Returning to the Palace, Zandro chatted pleasantly about his early days on the stage. He looked around Main Street with curiosity.

"I used to eat at that diner over there," he said. "I had little money in those days so my usual repast was a bowl of bean soup costing fifty cents. The owner was a theatergoer, though. He took pity on a young and struggling magician and would slip a hamburger before my eager eyes now and then. The small hotel next door, which is where I stayed, has been replaced by that gaudy gas station." He sighed. "So much has gone."

When they neared the Palace, Zandro stopped to look at the small group of people before the entrance. Magicians were unloading their equipment from automobiles and vans. "I shall say good-bye to you here," he said, shaking hands. "Only for the moment, though, because we will be seeing each other a great deal during the next few days. I am looking forward to meeting your renowned father. All of you will enjoy my performances, I am sure."

Then he strode past his rivals, his head high,

looking neither to left nor right. The others stared at him with obvious dislike, and a few remarks were said behind his back.

"I don't think he's going to be the most popular person in Bayport for the rest of the week," Joe predicted.

"Far from it," Frank agreed. "Uh-oh, here comes trouble!"

He was referring to Manuel, who had just walked out of the theater.

"There you are, you charlatan!" the little magician shouted, standing firmly in Zandro's path. "I've been waiting for you! How dare you slap your name on the poster?" He turned to the others, holding up the announcement. "Do you see this? Do you see how much nerve he has?"

Zandro glared down at his rival with contempt. "You fool!" he hissed. "This contest was my idea, you hear, mine! You complain that my name alone is on the poster? Who would come if it were not? I am the drawing card. I am nationally known." His lip curled. "Who would pay for a ticket if the name of some obscure amateur such as Manuel were on the poster? Rather than insulting me, you should be on your knees thanking me for the opportunity for displaying your meager talents."

"Thank you?" Manuel screamed. "What for? You only promoted this farce to puff yourself up. It was

24

going to be in Boston where you would be the kingpin and people would be fooled into thinking you were the best magician in the world. Then you heard I was entering so you set the theater on fire."

He waved a finger under the big man's nose. "You couldn't very well cancel it so you switched the show to this small city. You made sure I won't get too much national publicity when I defeat you."

Frank and Joe saw Zandro's face turn purple. With an obvious effort, he controlled himself from lashing out with his fists. He pushed past Manuel, saying haughtily, "I won't listen any more to these vicious lies!"

Infuriated, Manuel hurled himself at his enemy. There was a scuffle, but before Joe and Frank could separate the pair, Zandro jumped backwards.

"He's got a knife!" Zandro shouted. "He's trying to kill me!"

3 Strange Visitors

The boys rushed forward and stood between the antagonists. "What are you talking about?" Manuel cried. "I have never carried a knife in my life!"

"He's lying!" Zandro pointed at Manuel's left jacket pocket. "It's in there. He started taking it out when I jumped."

Manuel put his hand in his pocket. "Nonsense. I'll show—" The expression on his face changed from angry innocence to amazement as he took out a small gleaming blade. He stared at it, transfixed.

"You see," Zandro said with contempt, "what kind of people I am surrounded by? They are so full of jealousy that some would seek my life." He faced

27

the other magicians who had been looking on with their mouths open. "Is that not so, my friends?" he asked sardonically, laying emphasis upon the word *friends*.

"You can press charges, Zandro," Frank said. "We'll get a police officer and—"

Zandro waved away the suggestion. "I cannot be bothered. Ah, Happy, are we unpacked?"

The magician's manager had just come out of the entrance and was looking at everyone, confused. "What's going on?"

"This person—" Zandro indicated the glowering Manuel "—tried to kill me, that's all."

"Don't you see what he is trying to do?" Manuel asked, his dark eyes blazing. "He planted that knife in my pocket! Oh, he is clever, that one." He flung the weapon on the ground. "Here, take it! I'm leaving."

He turned and walked briskly down the street. Zandro looked after him with a sneer. Then he tucked his hand under Hortell's arm. "Come on, Happy, let us check out the equipment." Together they entered the theater.

"That's the craziest thing I've ever seen," a young, dark-haired magician said. "Manuel has a quick temper, but it usually disappears as quickly as it appears. I've never heard of him pulling a knife before."

28

"Do you think it really was his, Rumson?" another magician asked.

Rumson shrugged his shoulders. "It could have happened as Manuel said it did. It's the kind of thing Zandro would pull."

Joe and Frank introduced themselves. "Zandro was very polite to us," Joe said.

The magicians snorted. "You're not a threat to him," one of them said, "as we are. Though I don't really understand why."

"What do you mean?" Frank asked.

"He is what he says he is—the best," Rumson explained. "But he always seems afraid one of us is going to top him somehow. He's a very insecure guy."

"Insecure, huh?" another said. "Crazy out of his mind, I would call it. It's going to be some four days with Manuel and Zandro at each other's throats."

"But the money's good," Rumson said. "I can stand anything for a large fee. Well, let's get all this stuff in."

The magicians began carrying their equipment inside. Frank and Joe walked to their car.

"This may turn out to be more exciting than we thought," Joe commented as they headed home.

At five minutes after seven, Jack Wayne's car pulled up to the Hardy residence and Fenton Hardy got out.

Mrs. Hardy met him at the door. "You've come just in time," she said. "I was about to put dinner on the table."

"Could it wait just a few minutes?" her husband asked. "I would like to have a family conference first."

"Aunt Gertrude, too?"

"Absolutely."

Joe and Frank entered from the kitchen. They had been out in the Hardy laboratory above the garage, conducting an experiment. "What an afternoon we had, Dad," Joe exclaimed. "We met Zandro and—"

"Tell me later if you would, please," his father broke in. "Right now I have to talk to you all in the study."

Noting his serious expression, they followed him upstairs without comment. Once they were seated, though, Frank said, "Well, Dad?"

"Wait until your mother and aunt come," his father replied. A moment later, the two women arrived.

"You know the fish will be cold, Fenton," Aunt Gertrude scolded.

"I'm sorry," her brother said, "but this is of utmost importance." He smiled at her. "Even more important than your delicious cod cakes."

Half-appeased, she sat. "Well, if it doesn't take too long."

"I promise," he said. "As you know, I've been to Washington today. I have been given a secret assignment, so secret that I have been sworn to tell no one." He paused. "Not even my own family."

His listeners looked at one another. It was a rare occasion when the famous detective could not talk about a case.

"We understand," Mrs. Hardy said calmly.

"I have to tell you about some things, though," he continued. "Mr. Smith and Mr. Jones will arrive from Washington tomorrow and will be our guests for a few days."

"Mr. Smith and Mr. Jones, indeed." Aunt Gertrude sniffed. "Couldn't they think of better aliases than those?"

"They're convenient and easy," Mr. Hardy replied. "The men may seem, well, quiet to you, but please don't get the impression they are unfriendly. It's just that they have a lot on their minds and much to do."

He turned towards his sons.

"I'm afraid that you two will have to handle the security at the Palace without my help. I only wish Sam weren't on vacation; otherwise, he could give you a hand." The detective thought for a moment. "Maybe I could phone him and ask him to return."

"Don't do that, Dad," Frank protested. "You're the one who insisted that he take time off. He needs it badly."

"It's no great emergency," Joe added, "watching over things at the theater. We can handle it easily."

"And Ethel Radley has been looking forward to that cabin in the mountains," Mrs. Hardy said. "She really would be disappointed if they came back."

Fenton Hardy threw up his hands. "All right." He laughed. "I'm outnumbered. Ethel and Sam stay in the mountains."

Aunt Gertrude rose. "Now that that's settled, let's go to the table. There are some fine codfish cakes."

But Joe and Frank were not going to have the pleasure of enjoying their aunt's cooking immediately. On the way downstairs, they heard the hall phone ring. Frank picked it up. "Hello."

"Frank, this is Iola."

"I'd know your voice anywhere, Iola. How are you?"

"Frank, I thought you should know. I'm at the hospital and there's been an accident." There was an urgent tone to her voice. "Tony Prito has been brought into the emergency room with a broken leg."

"We'll be right over. Thanks." Frank hung up and relayed the news to Joe. They explained what had happened to the family, who were already sitting at the table.

"I think you could at least eat before going over to the hospital," Aunt Gertrude said, scowling. "They'll take a while to set the leg."

"He's one of their best friends, Gertrude," Fenton said. "Let them go. They can heat up the fish later."

Aunt Gertrude looked shocked at hearing this heresy from her brother's lips. "They don't eat enough as it is. Look at them—just skin and bones."

Mrs. Hardy looked over her sons' athletic frames. "I think they'll survive," she said dryly. "Go on, you two."

"How is it that Iola was at the hospital?" Frank inquired as they drove down Maple Street.

"Because she's a candy-striper volunteer," Joe said. "I thought you knew that."

Frank grinned. "No, I didn't, but then I don't keep up with her activities as closely as you do."

"Oh, go soak your head," Joe said good-naturedly.

In the waiting room of the Bayport Hospital, the youths found Mr. Prito, Police Chief Collig, his assistant, and Chet Morton.

"How is Tony?" Joe asked the contractor.

"It could have been a lot worse," Mr. Prito said. "He only broke his leg in one place. He might have broken his neck."

"How did it happen?" Frank asked.

33

"All we know is that he fell off the balcony and onto the stage."

"He was still at the theater?" Frank knit his brow. "Mr. Prito's crew usually quit at five o'clock."

"You know Tony. He loves to work. He wanted to put in an extra hour. He was in the opera house all alone."

"Iola phoned you, too, huh?" Joe said to Chet.

The heavyset youth shook his head. "No, I was the one who found Tony. We were going to a movie and I had driven to the opera house to pick him up. He was groaning, kind of out of his mind. Kept saying that someone had startled him or something like that. I couldn't make it all out."

"That's why I asked Chief Collig to drop by," said Mr. Prito. "Perhaps there was some unauthorized person in the theater."

Just then Iola entered the waiting room. "Dr. Kelly sent me to take you to Tony's room."

"How is he?" Mr. Prito asked as the group went up in the elevator.

"He seems all right," Iola replied. "He's not unconscious or anything like that."

Tony was lying in bed watching Dr. Kelly examine the cast on his right leg. He gave the visitors a rueful smile. "What a mess!" he said.

"How is he doing, Doc?" Mr. Prito asked the physician anxiously.

Dr. Kelly straightened up. "He'll live. It would have been better if he had landed on his head, though. He can't injure that thick skull." He gave them all a wink. "Seriously though, he'll be in here for a while."

Tony glared at the cast. "Will I be able to play football this fall?"

"We'll have to see about that," the doctor replied. "I think your chances are pretty good, however. You're young and healthy and the break was a clean one."

"Are you able to tell us what happened, Tony?" Chief Collig asked.

"I guess so," Tony said slowly. "It seems like a dream and some of it is kind of hazy."

"Just do your best," the police officer said, signalling to his assistant to start writing.

"Well, I was working late on the balcony. There is a rotting banister up there and I was taking it off so we could replace it with a new one tomorrow. Everybody else had gone home. It was very quiet except for the noise I was making."

Tony thought for a moment. "If I hadn't been making such a racket, pulling and hammering at the rotten wood, I might have heard him . . . it?" He looked puzzled. "The rest is confused and I don't really know what he or it is. Anyway, I'll tell you the rest if you don't laugh."

35

"No laughing," the police chief said seriously. "What happened?"

"All right. As I was going to say, I might have heard him coming if I hadn't made such a noise. Suddenly, there was a sound right behind me. I turned around and there was this . . . this thing. It was coming towards me, moaning. It glowed in the darkness. I know it sounds weird, but the thing was actually shining. I don't know if I was scared or not, but I sure was startled. I leaned back as it came, and the next thing I knew I was falling. That's all I can remember."

There was silence in the room as the listeners looked at each other.

"What do you think this thing was?" Chief Collig asked gently.

Tony gulped. "I didn't want to say it, but the thing looked like a man dressed in some strange clothes." He paused. "I think it was a ghost!"

4 *Mysterious Stakeout*

"A ghost?" Frank stared at Tony incredulously.

Tony shrugged. "I knew you wouldn't believe me. Well, I'm not saying it was a ghost. I don't know what it was, but it sure looked like one."

Tony could not shed any more light on the subject, and soon Dr. Kelly asked the visitors to leave. Chief Collig promised to check into the matter, then everyone went home.

While Frank and Joe had their late dinner, they told their family what had happened since Fenton Hardy had received the Washington phone call. They talked about Zandro, the visit to the old opera house, Jonathan Ridoux, the ghost of Alebert Cavendish, the knife incident, and finally Tony's explanation of his accident.

The detective frowned. "This affair at the opera house is not officially our business, but I hope something is being done about it."

"Well, Chief Collig is making a complete investigation," Joe said.

"Good. Now this magician tournament job may develop into a lot of trouble. Just watch yourselves and don't take any unnecessary risks. Now it's back to work for me. I have a lot of details to iron out before Mr. Smith and Mr. Jones get here tomorrow."

The men arrived at eight sharp the following morning. There were formal introductions all around, and Aunt Gertrude's face brightened when she discovered that they had had nothing to eat yet. They accepted her offer to make them eggs and bacon, but when they carried the food to their room on trays, she sat and ate her breakfast in grumpy silence. The boys were amused by her anger, but they didn't dare show it.

"What do you say that we look in at the Palace?" Frank suggested.

"All right," Joe said, "but let's drop in at the opera house first."

Four police cars were parked in front of the old building. A group of officers was gathered around Chief Collig, but most of them started to drift away towards their vehicles as Joe and Frank approached.

The chief looked annoyed. "We've been over the building with a fine tooth comb and didn't find a hint of a clue about Tony's assailant."

"You don't believe in the ghost theory, then, Chief?" Frank asked with a smile.

"Are you kidding? Oh, I think Tony saw a ghost all right, a real live one who is trying to get the work stopped."

"Say, did you hear about this Ridoux person?" Joe asked.

"Sure, he's our prime suspect. We would like to question him, but so far he's proved to be difficult to find. He's moved around from boardinghouse to boardinghouse so often. We'll catch up to him, though. One good thing—Mr. Prito is hiring a watchman."

The boys went on to the Palace and into the chaos that preceded the show. The magicians were practicing, stagehands were preparing for the eight-thirty opening, ropes and boxes lay around everywhere, and Mr. Heifitz had his ear glued to the phone as people called for reservations.

Frank and Joe decided that surveillance was impossible under such circumstances. They made their way once through the confusion, then had a long visit with Tony Prito at the hospital. They spent the remainder of the afternoon hauling compost for their mother's flower garden and tuning up their yellow sports sedan.

After an early supper, they started back to the Palace. When they had gone a block, Joe said, "Stop, Frank."

Frank pulled over to the curb. "What's up?"

Joe was looking back. "I noticed that black car parked a few yards from the house this afternoon, but I didn't pay much attention to it. It's still there, though. There are four men sitting in it and they seem to be watching our house."

Frank circled the block, came up behind the mysterious automobile, and parked. Joe, as Fenton Hardy had taught his sons, scribbled down the license number, making sure the men in the other car saw what he was doing. "They don't seem to be too worried," he remarked. "One of them even smiled at me."

"Well, Chief Collig can find out who the car belongs to," Frank said as they moved down the street again.

The scene at the Palace was more frantic than before. The audience was beginning to stream in, local people and magic fans from all over the country. The musicians of the orchestra were tuning up. The refreshment-stand workers were stacking cases of soft drinks in a corner of the foyer.

The noise backstage was deafening. It seemed that all the magicians were talking at the same time.

In the center of a circle was Zandro, Mr. Heifitz, Happy Hortell, Manuel, and the young magician, Rumson. Joe and Frank pushed through the crowd.

"You did it!" Happy Hortell looked anything but happy as he pointed an accusing finger at Manuel. "I saw you go into his dressing room about an hour ago."

"I didn't go in there to do any harm," Manuel shouted back. "I wanted to talk to him, that's all."

"Some story," Hortell snarled. "You waited until most of us had gone to supper. You didn't guess that I would be about."

"What's going on?" Frank inquired of Mr. Heifitz.

The theater manager was standing between Manuel and Hortell, looking helpless. "I'm so glad you've come. It seems that Rumson returned from supper to find that much of his equipment had been badly damaged or completely destroyed. Even his doves had been freed and have gone through a window. Mr. Hortell says that he saw Manuel go into Rumson's room."

"What he's done is disgraceful," Hortell yelled. "Send for the police, Heifitz!"

"You are a scoundrel," Manuel countered, "and you work for a scoundrel!"

"I can't believe this," Rumson said. "Why would Manuel want to do this to me?"

"Quiet!" Zandro bellowed. He had been standing

41

aside silently, observing the scene with a sardonic eye. His sudden shout made everyone jump and had the effect that he desired.

"That's better," he said when the group had fallen into startled silence. He looked at Rumson. "Young man," he rumbled, "you say you don't understand why this . . . this creature—" he waved in the direction of Manuel "—should have damaged your equipment. You are most naive due to your age and relative inexperience in how vicious professional jealousy can be."

"Professional jealousy!" Manuel spluttered. He was unable to utter another sound for he choked in fury.

"It is obvious why *he* did such a deed," Zandro went on, ignoring Manuel's outburst. "He knows that he cannot possibly defeat me in the coming contest, but he does hope for second place, which, after all, is worth a considerable sum of money as well as national recognition. However, you have some talent, more than he, and he is concerned that you might win the coveted second place. Ergo, he used this underhanded way to eliminate you."

All listened to this theory in amazement. Some nodded in agreement.

"But," Zandro thundered, holding up a finger, "I shall not allow him to profit from this crime. Happy Hortell shall take you to my dressing room and there you shall choose the equipment you need."

The others gasped at this act of generosity. Zandro wrapped his cloak about him. "Of course," he added, "I shall expect you to return what you borrow."

He strode off. "What a man!" Hortell breathed.

"What an exit!" one of the magicians said.

Manuel recovered his voice. "What a liar!" He clenched his fists. "Someday I will kill him!" He turned to Rumson. "I am innocent of all this. That is all I have to say." Then he, too, left.

The show must have been a good one, according to the sound of applause and cheering, but Joe and Frank didn't see any of it. They were patrolling backstage all the time, making sure there would be no repetition of the break-in of Rumson's dressing room.

When all the participants had completed their acts, the judges announced their decision. Eight magicians had been eliminated, and eight would go into the second round. Among the survivors were Zandro, Manuel, and Rumson.

After the curtain dropped, the magicians changed and left hurriedly. The last to depart was Manuel. When he passed Frank and Joe, who were checking off those who were leaving on a clipboard, he snarled, "I know you! You're Zandro's stooges!"

"Hold it a minute," Frank said angrily. "We have

only one job to do here. We are responsible for security, for seeing that everything is going along smoothly. We are not stooges for anyone!"

"Well, things are *not* going along smoothly," the small, dark man snapped. "I've been accused of committing a horrendous deed and you stood listening to Zandro, nodding your heads in agreement."

"We didn't nod our heads," Joe said indignantly, but he was too late, for the magician had rushed through the exit and out of earshot.

Frank patted his brother's back. "Don't get excited. Manuel will probably be saying things like that for the next three days."

Mr. Heifitz appeared from the front office. "Time to lock up. Everyone out?"

Joe looked down at the list. "All gone, sir."

The three of them walked to the front entrance, and the theater manager turned off lights as they went.

"We did have that early spot of trouble," Mr. Heifitz said, locking the street door. "But it was a packed house and I think we'll have a most profitable week. Although I confess I'll be happy when it is all over."

The weary youths drove down Main Street, anxious to get home and to bed. Frank glanced at the opera house and then pulled to the curb.

"What's up?" Joe asked sleepily.

44

"There's a light moving around in there." Frank pointed at the theater.

"It's probably the watchman," Joe said. "After all, he can't walk around in the dark."

"Just the same, I think we should investigate."

They crossed the street and Frank tried the door. To their surprise, it opened. "Not very smart to keep that unlocked," he commented.

They entered cautiously. "Where's the light that you saw?" Joe asked.

"Gone." Frank advanced a few steps. Then Joe heard him gasp.

"What happened, Frank?"

"Tripped over something. Do you have your light?"

Joe took out his thin-beam flashlight and pointed it down at Frank's feet. "It's a man!"

5 *The Intruder*

"It's the watchman!" Frank cried as they stared at the uniformed man with the emblem CARTER SECU-RITY SERVICE emblazoned on the upper right side of his shirt.

The victim groaned and opened his eyes. He looked at them with terror. "Don't hit me again," he croaked.

"Take it easy," Joe advised. "We didn't do this to you."

The watchman made an attempt to rise, but the effort was too much and he fell back.

"Don't move," Frank said. He took off his jacket, folded it, and slipped it under the man's head. "Do you know who hurt you?"

46

"Didn't hear a thing," the watchman said, "until he was on top of me. He sneaked up from behind." He frowned in puzzlement. "He was—shining. At least, that's what I saw in a flash before he hit me. And he was dressed in funny clothes."

Joe glanced at his brother. "The ghost of Alebert Cavendish," the younger Hardy stated in a quiet voice.

"Ghost?" The watchman looked frightened. "He was a ghost?"

"If he were a ghost, he wouldn't have hit you," Frank said dryly. "A real ghost would just scare you to death."

The man was not convinced. "He *could* have been a ghost," he said slowly. "He certainly looked like one."

Suddenly, from backstage came the sound of wood being chopped. "You stay there," Frank whispered to the watchman. "Don't try to get up. We'll be back soon."

"Don't leave me," the man pleaded.

"You'll be all right for a few minutes," Joe said. "We're going to get the ghost." Holding the pencil-thin light, he led the way along the middle aisle. The two youths cautiously went up the stairs and onto the stage. They would have crossed it success-fully if it had not been for a short two-by-four that a careless worker had left on the floor. Frank tripped over it and fell heavily.

47

Immediately, the chopping sound stopped. Joe snapped off his flashlight and the boys froze. They remained perfectly still for a long minute, but the noise did not resume.

"I guess he heard us and got away," Frank said. "Let's see what he did."

They walked further back towards the other side of the stage and came upon a scene of wreckage! The ghost had done his work well—almost all the reconstruction had been smashed with an axe that still lay on the floor.

"Mr. Prito will be very upset!" Joe predicted and leaned down to pick up the axe.

"Nothing to be done now," Frank said grimly. "We'd better go back to the watchman."

They turned to retrace their steps when there was a bloodcurdling scream. Suddenly, a luminous apparition stood before them. Its face was greenish and its body gave off a phosphorescent shimmer. The figure pointed at them with a long, bony finger. "Go!" it boomed at them. "Go and never return! This is the theater of the dead. The living have no place here."

As accustomed as the boys were to reacting immediately in the face of danger, they were momentarily immobilized by the ghastly figure before them. They quickly recovered, though, and rushed at the intruder. The shining apparition vanished at that moment. To their amazement, they grasped

air. Only a long throaty chuckle floated through the old theater, fading away. Joe flashed his light around them.

"Point it up," Frank requested. Joe did so and the thin beam caught a rope swinging idly above the place where the vandal had appeared. "That's how he escaped after turning off the lights he must wear under his outfit. He just swung away."

"Listen," Joe said. Frank strained his ears until he, too, heard faint steps behind them.

"He's going backstage again," Frank said.

"And up the stairs to the balcony," Joe added.

They moved as quietly and quickly as they could in the direction from where the sounds had come. When they arrived at the top of the balcony stairs, they heard a door slam.

"Down this way," Frank said. Giving up all attempts at silence, they ran along the corridor. "Here it is."

Joe's light shone on the door. "Room number 13. It's the dressing room that Zandro showed us."

They went into the room, prepared to rush the trespasser . . . but no one was there! "And no windows," Joe observed.

"The closet," Frank said, pointing. He pulled open the door. "Empty!"

"He left something behind." Joe stooped and picked up a worn slipper.

"How did he escape? The walls seem solid enough."

"Ghosts can do anything," Joe said.

Frank frowned. "Now don't you start that, too. If it really were a ghost, then it shouldn't have to open a door. It would walk right through the wall."

Joe chuckled. "Oh, I don't believe in ghosts. But you have to admit that whoever he is, he's pretty clever."

"It would be funny," Frank said, "if he wasn't going around hitting people and smashing up the theater. That costume would be just right at Halloween."

They made a futile search of the other dressing rooms, and then returned to the front entrance where the injured watchman was standing up wobbily.

"We'll call for an ambulance," Frank offered. "Put your arm around my shoulder and—"

He waved them off. "No, thanks. I can manage. I'm going home. Enough is enough. I don't mind guarding anything against *people*, but I draw the line when it comes to ghosts. I'm quitting!"

No amount of persuasion could make him change his mind. The boys accompanied him out to his car and saw him drive away. Then they phoned the police and Mr. Prito from a street corner booth to inform them of what had happened.

Two patrol cars arrived at the theater within three minutes. "You're the Hardys, aren't you?" a white-haired officer asked, then introduced himself as Dan Corey. "I was here this morning when you came. So we've got more trouble." He shook his head. "Who wants to mess up this old building? Doesn't seem to be any reason. Chief Collig sure isn't going to like this when he hears about it tomorrow."

"It certainly is strange," Frank agreed.

Mr. Prito's automobile pulled to the curb. "It's lucky you boys were here," he commented as he joined the group. He looked around. "Where's the watchman?"

"I'm afraid he's left for good," Joe said and explained how the man had been frightened of ghosts.

The contractor snorted. "He's a big help. Now what am I going to do? I want to catch this vandal before he does anything else, not only for the sake of the job, but for what he did to Tony."

"I think we ought to start going through the theater, Mr. Prito," the white-haired policeman said. "You never can tell. Maybe he's hiding in there somewhere."

"I doubt it, Dan," Mr. Prito said grumpily. He nodded towards Frank and Joe. "If they didn't find him, he's left. But I suppose we ought to try, anyhow."

They took a half-hour to go through the old building. At the end, Mr. Prito shrugged. "Just as I thought—no clues. For all we know, he may be watching us from outside, waiting for us to leave. Then he's going to continue wrecking."

Frank pulled Joe aside and conferred with him for a moment. "It's all right with me," Joe said.

"Mr. Prito, we'll be glad to stay here for the rest of the night," Frank said.

"That's really good of you," Tony's father answered. "Ordinarily, I would refuse, but I'm getting desperate. This crazy nut has set our work back a week at least. If we don't stop him, someone may be killed. You be careful, hear?"

"We will," Frank promised and turned to Officer Corey. "Could you do us a favor?"

"It depends on what it is."

Frank handed him a piece of paper. "Here's a license number. Would you ask Chief Collig to trace it so we can learn who owns the car?"

"I'll be glad to do that. I'm getting off patrol before the chief arrives, but I'll leave a note on his desk where he'll be sure to see it when he comes in."

When the police and Mr. Prito had left, the boys phoned home. They spoke to Mrs. Hardy, saying they were keeping an eye on the opera house until morning. They did not mention the ghost, though, since they did not want to worry her. Then they locked the front door of the theater and walked up on the stage. Frank looked at his watch. "Almost one o'clock. Suppose I stand watch until four-thirty, and you take the rest."

"Okay," Joe said. He lay down, put his head on his jacket for a pillow, and was asleep within a minute.

"Rise and shine." Joe shook his older brother gently. "The sun's up."

"What time is it?"

"Seven on the head and the crew is beginning to arrive."

Frank got up gingerly. "Concrete isn't any harder than this stage. It's a good thing we can go home now." He grinned. "I expect that the ghost has gone to bed. They sleep in the daytime, you know."

"So I've heard," Joe said dryly.

A light fog had settled over the port city, and Frank drove slowly with the lights on. As they went down Elm Street, they kept a sharp eye out for the mysterious black limousine, but it was nowhere to be seen.

When they approached the front of the garage and Frank reached for the button to open the doors, Joe cried out, "Hey! Look there!"

They saw a figure slip around the corner of the building. The two youths were out of the automobile in a flash, but they halted when they reached the back of the garage and peered through the fog. "There he goes!" yelled Frank, catching sight of the trespasser dashing into the property in the rear of the Hardy residence.

They gave chase, but were too late. The man had a car parked on Maple Street. He jumped into it, the engine roared, and the vehicle disappeared into the fog!

6 Threatening Notes

Fenton Hardy was making coffee and frying eggs when the boys entered the kitchen. Mr. Jones was sitting at the table, saying, "When the plane arrives from Washington, we'll have secret—" but he stopped when he saw Frank and Joe. He nodded to them amicably, rose, took the tray extended to him by Mr. Hardy, and looked at the bacon and eggs and the two cups of steaming coffee. "Terrific!" he said. "Thanks. See you later." He disappeared, and momentarily they could hear him mounting the stairs up to the guest room.

"You two are up early," Mr. Hardy said to his sons.

"Slight correction, Dad," Joe said, opening the

refrigerator and taking out orange juice and milk. "We're home late."

They narrated the strange events of the night. "And as we came home, we saw someone hanging around the garage," Frank finished. "We chased him to Maple Street, but he jumped into a car and got away. It was too foggy to get the license-plate number."

Fenton Hardy opened his mouth to comment just as the phone rang. He frowned and picked it up. "Hello? Yes, this is Fenton Hardy. Oh, hello." His face lit up as he recognized an old friend. He silently mouthed the words "Mr. Prito" at his sons. "I hear there's been more trouble at the opera house. You can't get any guards and you wish us to take over the night security? Well, I don't know. I'm involved in a day-and-night case, Sam is away on vacation, and Frank and Joe are helping out at the Palace during the magician tournament." He glanced at his sons who were frantically gesturing. "Tell you what. I'll see if I can make arrangements. I'll let you know. Oh, sure, I'll call you today. Right. Best to Tony. Good-bye."

After hanging up, he asked, "What do you two have in mind?"

"It's just this, Dad," Frank said excitedly. "Only one of us is needed at the Palace. Either Joe or I can stay at the opera house."

57

Fenton Hardy sat and sipped his coffee. He was lost in thought for a moment. "Maybe one of you can handle the job at the Palace, although I'm not quite sure, considering the threat of knives and the smashing of equipment. But even if you could convince me of that, I certainly do not believe that a single person could take on being watchman at the opera house. Two people have already been hurt, one seriously. This ghost is a dangerous person."

"Well, would you agree to two persons at the opera house?" Joe asked. "I could get Chet Morton."

Fenton raised his eyebrows dubiously. "Chet? Do you really think he's up to it?"

"Sure, he is," Joe defended their close friend.

"I'll rely on your judgment, then. I certainly would like to help Mr. Prito. After you've checked with Chet, tell me what he said." He finished his coffee and got up. "I'll be up in my study."

Chet's usually cheerful voice was laced with sleepiness as he answered the phone. "Watiz?" he managed to murmur. Joe explained how he had volunteered his friend to stand watch at the opera house. "You must be kidding!" Chet protested. "That kind of work is not my line!"

"Come on, Chet, it will be fun," Joe teased.

"You have a strange idea of fun," Chet grumbled. "I know you don't believe in ghosts, but I like to keep an open mind on the subject."

Joe laughed. "Don't worry. I know you can outrun any spirit."

It took five more minutes of persuasion, but in the end Chet reluctantly agreed.

"Come over here late this afternoon," Joe said and hung up before his friend could change his mind.

Frank and Joe finished breakfast and ascended to the study serving as their father's office. The detective nodded when Joe told him that Chet was willing to help guard, and then phoned Mr. Prito to tell him the news.

When he hung up, he said, "Well, that's settled. Now I'd like you to come with me." He led the way to the guest room and knocked. "This is Fenton," he called.

They heard steps, and then the door was unlocked. Jones peeked out. "I want you to hear about something that happened to the boys when they came home this morning," Mr. Hardy said.

Jones turned his head and called to the other man in the room, "Cover the papers." He waited a moment, and then opened the door wide. "Come in."

A bridge table was filled with documents that had been turned over. Smith sat there, obviously annoyed at being interrupted. His expression changed, though, as Frank and Joe narrated the incident of the shadowy figure.

"Didn't you get a good look at him?" Jones asked.

"No, it was hard to see through the fog," Frank said. "The fog also made it impossible to read the license plate or to tell exactly what kind of a car he was driving."

The tension was like electricity in the room as the three men looked at each other.

"Who do you think it could be?" Smith inquired of Fenton Hardy.

The detective held up a hand, then turned to his sons. "That will be all," he said curtly. "Both of you ought to get some sleep. You've had a long night, and there may be a tougher one ahead of you."

The boys left. They were slightly resentful at being dismissed that way, but they knew their father would let them know someday what this was all about.

They slipped into their beds and fell asleep immediately. When Aunt Gertrude knocked on their door to say Chief Collig was phoning, they were surprised to discover it was one o'clock in the afternoon. Frank put on a bathrobe and went out to the hall phone.

"I heard you and Joe are going to take over the night security at the opera house, so I thought you would be interested to learn that Jonathan Ridoux has completely disappeared. We finally tracked down his present boardinghouse, but he hasn't been seen there lately. If he does show up at the theater, try to hold him and call us."

"Right, Chief, will do."

"Oh, one other thing, Frank. About that car license you asked us to check on. Well, we did. It's a dead end. I'm sorry, but we were told that knowing the ownership is privileged information. The State Department of Vehicles won't even give us a hint."

"Well, thanks anyhow, Chief."

"I guess that's that," Joe said when Frank told him what Chief Collig had said. "As for the opera house trouble, do you really think that Ridoux is the ghost? That man we chased was pretty quick. Ridoux looked as if he could hardly walk, much less run."

"I'll admit it seems far-fetched," Frank agreed, "but at the moment he's the most logical suspect. Perhaps he hired someone to wreck the theater."

"He didn't appear as if he had a lot of money. His clothes were old and he lived in various boarding-houses."

"He wouldn't be the first old man to hoard his cash," Frank pointed out. "Say, who's going to work at the Palace tonight?"

"I thought we could flip a coin. Heads, I get the Palace, tails, you do."

"It's all right by me," Frank said. "Flip away."

Joe tossed a quarter in the air. It landed on the

rug. "Heads," Joe said. "I get the magicians, you get the ghost."

"Very funny," Frank said.

The brothers spent the remainder of the afternoon theorizing about the disappearance of the ghost. They could not come up with an answer that satisfied them, though, and were relieved when they heard a cheerful, familiar voice.

"Well, here I am!" The round face of Chet Morton grinned at them from the door.

"Just in time," Frank said, glancing at his watch. "Five on the nose. And I'm glad your attitude seems to have changed from this morning."

Chet laughed. "I decided you were right. I can run faster than any old ghost. Anyhow, the summer's become kind of dull. This opera house caper breaks up the monotony."

"Here's the schedule," Joe said as they drove downtown. "I'm dropping you and Frank off at the opera house and I'm going to the Palace. When I'm through there, I'm going to pick up some hamburgers and bring them to you. Then I'll leave the car there and walk home."

"Okay," Chet said. "Just don't forget the hamburgers."

The magician tournament went off smoothly. The judges eliminated all but four of them. Zandro and Manuel were among the survivors. Joe believed that the bitter rivals were equal in skill. The other two, which included Rumson, were far behind.

Even when the men left, there was no problem, although Manuel glared silently at Joe as he went out the exit.

Only Happy Hortell seemed nervous. Waiting for Zandro, who was, as usual, the last to leave, the manager paced up and down the hallway with his eyes on the floor, deep in thought. Now and then, he glanced at Joe. Finally, he said, "I'd like to talk to you a minute. Zandro will be very angry, but this has gone too far. This is the very first time I have ever disobeyed his orders, but it is wrong not to tell you—*very* wrong."

"What is, Mr. Hortell?" Joe asked.

Happy Hortell looked around to see if anyone else was in sight. Then his voice dropped to a conspiratorial whisper. "Zandro's been getting threatening letters, terrible letters."

Joe frowned. "Threatening letters? What do they threaten?"

"To kill him!"

7 Plunge into Space

"He just laughs at the threats," Hortell continued, "but I'm worried. I'm afraid of the things that have been happening. I'm afraid of Manuel."

"You were right to inform me of this," Joe said. "I'll tell my father and—"

Just then Zandro swept out of his dressing room, his cape flowing behind him. He looked at them with an amused expression. "What are you two plotting?"

"You really should have told us about receiving threatening letters," Joe said severely.

The magician shrugged. "You were hired to protect the theater, my young detective. Threats against me don't seem to have any bearing on your work."

"They certainly do," Joe retorted grimly. "If you are injured or worse, that would effectively end the magician tournament and we were hired by Mr. Heifitz to prevent that."

Zandro nodded. "You argue well. I'll cooperate. I must tell you, though, that I don't take such threats seriously. I've been receiving them all my life."

"Could I see the letters?" Joe persisted.

"Unfortunately, Joseph, I destroyed them. I promise you, though, that should I receive any additional ones, I shall of course notify you and—"

"He got one this afternoon," Hortell said excitedly, "and threw it away, but I managed to take it out of the garbage." Aware of the magician's angry glare, he added apologetically, "I'm sorry, Zandro, but these notes could be serious. I would not like to see you hurt, my friend, or, as Joe said, worse."

He dug a crumpled piece of paper from his back pocket and handed it to Joe. The message was short, simple, and to the point: I SHALL KILL YOU, YOU FAT SHAM!

"I do resent the term 'fat'," Zandro said, smiling. "I would prefer 'portly.'"

Ignoring the star's banter, Joe asked, "How did you get this? By mail?"

"It was slipped under the dressing-room door," Happy Hortell answered. "We found it when we came at five to get ready for the show."

"They have always been delivered when we were

out," Zandro said. "It appears that the writer is very aware of my schedule and habits." He looked at Joe meaningfully.

"You believe that this is an inside job, that someone in the show or connected with the Palace has been delivering these notes?" Joe said.

"I can draw no other conclusion," Zandro said grandly.

"I'd like to keep this, if you don't mind."

"I have no further use for it," Zandro said, looking at the paper with disgust. "And now I think we shall depart. Come, Happy."

When the two had walked through the exit, Joe made a fast check of the dressing rooms. Then he ran to the front office. Mr. Heifitz, slipping the night's receipts into a canvas bag, looked up in surprise. "I thought you had already gone, Joe," he remarked.

"No. I think we have another problem," Joe said and told the manager about the threats. "Mr. Heifitz, do you have any samples of the writing of the people who are in the show?"

The theater man thought a moment, then snapped his fingers. "Of course! I have a form that all performers must fill out. I have to send it to the Internal Revenue Service for tax purposes." He opened a drawer and pulled out a sheaf of papers.

Joe thumbed through the pile until he came to

Manuel's form. Looking on, Mr. Heifitz remarked, "It does seem logical to check on him first."

"But the handwriting doesn't seem to be the same, does it?" Joe compared the threatening note with every form, even Zandro's.

"You don't possibly believe he would have written those letters to himself?" Mr. Heifitz, asked, mildly shocked.

"No, I really don't, but stranger things have happened." Joe sighed as he handed the forms back. "None of these match."

"You must remember that you are dealing with magicians," said Mr. Heifitz. "I imagine all of them are clever enough to disguise their handwriting."

"I'll take the note to the police. Maybe they will be able to spot a clue."

The cloudy weather had cleared and the night sky sparkled with stars. Joe took a deep breath of the fresh clean air, a relief from the close atmosphere of the theater. Then he got into the yellow sports sedan and turned the key.

Immediately, he heard a whirring sound from beneath the hood. Joe dived out of the open door and hit the pavement. There was an explosion, and he covered his head with his hands to protect himself from flying debris. Yet, there weren't any pieces of dangerous metal tearing through the air and no fire. Suddenly, all was still again. Only an acrid smell remained.

After waiting five minutes, Joe rose and gingerly opened the hood. Attached to a spark plug was a fake bomb—really a noisemaker that let off smoke. He recognized it as a device that was sometimes sold in trick shops and was still used by magicians. The "bomb" was cool and he detached it with a handkerchief; it might, he thought, have fingerprints. He put it in the trunk and got back into the car.

On the passenger side, he found a message. When he switched on his pocket flashlight, he noticed that the handwriting was the same as that in Zandro's threatening letter. YOU KIDS STOP NOSING AROUND THE PALACE OR NEXT TIME IT WILL BE A REAL BOMB!

"Thanks for the warning," Joe said, starting the engine.

He stopped at Pete's Diner and bought four hamburgers, an order of french fries, and two soft drinks. Then he continued to the opera house.

As Joe was approaching the theater, Chet burst through the front doors with a look of panic on his face. He crashed into Joe, sending food and drinks high in the air.

"Joe," the terrified youth shouted. "Frank has disappeared!"

Nothing unusual had occurred during the first few hours at the opera house. Frank and Chet had made a tour every hour throughout the entire theater.

They had just finished their midnight check and were relaxing on cots, which they had set up on the stage. Chet had closed his eyes and was sinking into a light sleep while Frank was reading a book by the light of a battery-operated lamp.

Suddenly, the ghost dashed out from the wings towards them! It grabbed their cots almost simultaneously and overturned them. Both boys were thrown into the orchestra pit; the ghost hurled the lamp far into the seats where it smashed into darkness. Then, with a howl, their attacker moved backstage again.

"Come on, let's get him!" Frank yelled.

"Don't you think we ought to call the cops?" Chet quavered, but Frank was already scrambling back up to the stage. Chet reluctantly climbed after him and started to crawl around on the floor.

"What are you doing?" Frank asked.

"Looking for our flashlights."

"No time now," the Hardy boy said. "That creep probably kicked them somewhere. We'll have to follow the sound."

Frank moved forward without worrying that he might fall. Fenton Hardy had trained his sons to thoroughly memorize layouts of rooms and buildings in case they had to go through them in the dark. Now Frank heard the ghost move up the stairs.

There was a dull, heavy thud and a cry of pain behind him. "I fell, Frank," Chet called.

"He went up to the balcony," hissed Frank. "I'm going up."

Silently, he slipped up the steps and stopped at the top. His ears caught the faint sounds of the attacker moving towards the dressing rooms. A door creaked open and then shut. Frank knew what room had been entered. You're back in room number 13, Mr. Ghost, the boy thought to himself, and I'm going to get you this time.

He stood at the entrance of the dressing room and listened intently for the sound of breathing. There was none, but suddenly there came a click as the closet door closed.

Frank was across the room in two strides and into the closet, his arms flailing. As before, there was no one there.

"You're not going to get away so easily this time," Frank said and gritted his teeth. He felt around the three walls without result. He was about to give up in frustration when his hand touched a coat hook. Immediately, the back panel gave way.

Frank stepped ahead cautiously, testing the boards beneath him before putting his entire weight upon them. He realized that he was on a small landing. He squatted and reached out to his right. Steps! Apparently, there were stairs leading upwards.

He felt around with his left hand and discovered stairs going downward. As he stood and wondered which way to go, a groan wafted up from below.

Slowly, Frank went down the stairs. Whoever was at the bottom obviously wasn't aware of him because the groans continued.

Then Frank took one step too many. The stairs ended and he plunged into black space!

8 The Secret Room

Frank landed as he had been trained—as a paratrooper hits the earth. He rolled over and over. When he finished moving, he listened carefully. The groans continued.

"Can I help you?" Frank asked.

"Light . . . light," said the whispered voice.

"I don't have a light."

"In back of you . . . by the wall."

Frank groped in the dark and finally touched a metal object. He pushed a switch and light blazed out from a battery-operated lantern.

He slowly moved the light around in a circle. The walls were made of cinderblock; there were no doors or windows. He heard a click above, and turned the light upwards, but saw only the broken stairs several feet from the ground and the darkness beyond. Then he brought the lantern down to see the groaning figure lying in the center of the room. He was only mildly surprised to see that the ghost was Jonathan Ridoux.

In the meantime, Chet had stumbled backstage, falling several times, and then up the stairs to the balcony. He stopped there, uncertain which way to turn. He held his breath for a full minute, straining to hear the slightest sound.

"Frank!" he said. There was no answer. "Frank!" he repeated, more loudly. Again silence. "FRANK!" he shouted this time, but only his echo replied.

He retreated down the stairs. His journey to the front of the theater was a series of bumps, trips, and falls. At last, he saw the faint light from under the front doors. He ran out at top speed and crashed into Joe, who was arriving with their food.

After the younger Hardy had managed to calm his friend down to the point where Chet could relate a fairly coherent story, the two retraced the path to the backstage balcony.

"You heard Frank up here?" Joe asked.

"No, no, he *told* me he was going up," Chet corrected. "I didn't hear him. You know how quietly he moves."

Joe and Chet checked the entire balcony from the

73

area where Tony had fallen to the last dressing room. Joe made an especially careful inspection of room 13, including the closet, but the walls seemed solid and he did not pull on the coat hook that had opened the secret entrance for Frank.

Dejectedly, the two boys descended the balcony stairs. "Well, I guess all we can do now is call the police," Joe said tensely, "and have them go over the whole place again."

Neither of them noticed a tall thin figure by the exit door since they were moving in the other direction. As soon as Joe's flashlight shone up the aisle, the stranger slipped out of the door into the alley.

There another figure awaited him. "*What* is going on?" asked the man.

There was a low chuckle. "Better than we thought. The stairs to the basement gave way just where we had sawed them when Ridoux came running down. He's trapped in there for good. No one can hear him from the dressing room."

"I wish we could have used Ridoux further," the other man said. "But I suppose it's just as well. He might have been caught and brought the police down on our heads, and our little scheme would have been uncovered."

"But Ridoux doesn't really know anything," the tall, thin man observed, "so what could he have told the police?"

"They'd have put two and two together," his accomplice said with a trace of annoyance, "and if they hadn't, those Hardy boys would've."

"One of them, perhaps," the thin man said triumphantly, "but not that older one."

"Frank?"

"Yes. Somehow he found out how to get through the closet. But he didn't have a flashlight. He went down the stairs and fell as Ridoux did."

"Are you sure?"

"Positive. I crept to the landing and heard the two of them talking. Then Hardy got hold of Ridoux's lantern and I decided it was time to go. I had just reached the exit when I heard Joe Hardy and some other guy coming through the theater so I stuck around to see what they were up to. They went looking all through the dressing rooms for Frank, but they never stumbled on the secret exit."

"Where are they now?"

"On their way to call the police."

"Then I suggest that we leave with caution, but with haste, before the constabulary arrives."

The search party was the largest that had ever gone through the opera house. There were twenty police officers, Chief Collig, Mr. Prito, and Fenton Hardy. Deep rings under the contractor's eyes showed his exhaustion and anxiety. Mr. Hardy, who had hastily put on slacks and an old sweater when Joe phoned him, looked angry. Chief Collig wasted no time. He barked orders and his men jumped into action.

The theater was completely lit with spotlights. Not a corner was overlooked. After an hour, though, the chief shook his head in frustration. "Not a clue! Just like the last two times."

But Frank just didn't disappear into thin air," Fenton stated. "Either he's been spirited out of the building or he's still somewhere inside."

Collig nodded. "Hidden somewhere, but where?"

"Well, we just can't give up," the private detective said grimly.

"And we won't," the police officer added. "But I'll have to release half my group so they can go back to their regular duties." He scowled. "Unfortunately, crime continues to go on in the rest of the city."

"I understand, Chief," Fenton said calmly. "I appreciate all you're trying to do."

"I'll tell you one thing," Mr. Prito said. "My company will do no more work in this place until all this is cleared up. It's worse than being in a war!"

"Only up to now, no one has been killed," Collig observed.

"As far as we know," Fenton said. "Suppose we start examining the building from the outside."

"Good idea," the police chief said. "I don't see what more we can accomplish inside."

"It seems as if you have a broken leg," Frank said

after carefully examining Jonathan Ridoux.

The would-be actor gripped his knee. "Oh, why did this happen to me?" he groaned.

"As my Aunt Gertrude would say, it serves you right," Frank said. "Because of you, Tony Prito also has a broken leg and is in the hospital. And it was just lucky that that watchman doesn't have a fractured skull."

"It wasn't me, it wasn't me!"

"What do you mean, it wasn't you?" Frank cried out, pointing at the odd costume that Ridoux was wearing. "There are lights underneath that outfit that you switch on when you want to scare someone."

"I know I did those things," the elderly man said, his eyes rolling wildly, "but I was ordered to."

"Ordered to? Who ordered you to?"

Ridoux's voice rose almost to a shriek. "The ghosts, the ghosts!"

Frank looked at the man closely. There was no mistaking Ridoux's sincerity, especially considering his great pain. "Where did you see the ghosts?" Frank asked gently.

"They came one night to my room in the boardinghouse. They stood by my bed and told me I must stop the restoration. They said it was a blasphemy."

"Did you know who these ghosts were?"

"Oh, yes. The thin one was John Barrymore and the heavy one was Charles Laughton. They gave me this costume and told me how to turn the lights on and off. It's all done with a battery." He smiled in spite of his pain. "They didn't know about this room, though. I told them about it."

"Why did they want you to stop the restoration? Why not frighten off the workers themselves?"

"Oh, they explained that," said Ridoux. "They have no physical strength so they needed me to do the damage."

"If they have no physical strength, then how did they manage to saw through the stairs?" Frank inquired.

"They couldn't have done that!"

Frank stood up and held the lantern near the broken stairs. "The risers were cut nearly all the way through. It was planned that when you came down, the stairs would fall apart." He lowered the lantern to the floor. "Here's the sawdust. I never heard of ghosts doing this."

Ridoux shook his head. "It wasn't the ghosts. It was someone else, maybe your brother or your friend."

"You know better than that. No one but you and the ghosts knew where this room was." Seeing that the old man remained unconvinced, Frank said, "Go on with your story."

Ridoux shrugged. "That's about it. The ghosts gave me a key to the rear door so I could come and go as I pleased. All I wanted to do was to chop up the work with an axe and frighten the people. I never thought that young man would fall off the balcony."

"I can believe that, but what about the watchman? You certainly gave him a clout."

"Oh, that was an accident, too. I did have this iron bar. I only wanted to scare him with it. I held it high over my head when I sneaked up behind him. But he turned around suddenly and gave me such a start that I dropped the bar, which hit him on the head. When he fell, I picked the bar up and ran." He looked remorseful.

Frank wondered what the watchman would say if he knew how much he had scared a ghost.

"You almost caught me that time," Ridoux continued. "I had just gone through the closet panel when you and your brother came into the dressing room. I stood on the landing, not daring to breathe while you two made your search."

"Where are we, anyway?" Frank asked, holding up the lantern and examining the walls.

Ridoux's eyes lit up as he saw a chance to talk about his favorite subject—the history of the Bayport Opera House. "A long time ago, the dressing rooms were little more than portable stalls set up in the wings. There was no backstage balcony then. Open stairs came down to this room where props

79

were stored. If you had taken the stairs up, you would have reached a large room under the roof. You can see it from outside. It's shaped like a dome. Costumes were stored in that room."

Frank looked at the broken stairs, realizing that he could not reach them. "Is there another way out of here?"

"None!"

Frank sighed, realizing how hopeless escape seemed. Perhaps if Ridoux stood on his shoulders, the elderly man could pull himself up on the end of the stairs. But the old man was frail and, besides, he could never stand on his broken leg.

Frank shook a little and rubbed his arms. "It's cool in here."

"It's always been cool," Ridoux said. "In mid-summer, I would find my way here to escape the heat and read."

"There's a draft!" Frank yelled.

"I'm sorry," said Ridoux sympathetically. "Perhaps if you move to another side of the room, you won't feel it."

"But I want to feel it! Where is it coming from?" For two minutes, Frank toured the room, turning and twisting in an attempt to trace the slight elusive breeze. Finally, he put his hand on the wall. "It's coming from here. This cinderblock is loose. Some of the mortar around it has worn away."

Ridoux looked at the youth in wonder, forgetting

all about his pain. "Do you feel all right?"

Frank was too excited to answer. He rummaged through the wreckage of the stairs until he found a sharp piece of wood. Then he began to jab at the weak mortar.

"Let's hope we're lucky," he said to Ridoux. "If this doesn't work, we may be here forever!"

9 The Captive Reporter

Frank continued to scratch desperately at the loose mortar while Jonathan Ridoux babbled on and on.

"Oh, this theater has seen great days, great days! The stars who trod on its boards! Gillette, Edwin Booth, Maude Adams, so many others. And the theater managers, all of them magnificent. Of course, some of them were eccentric." He chuckled. "John Harrison, for example. You remember him, don't you? He was manager from 1890 to 1920."

Frank stepped back from his work to rest a moment. He had been listening half-heartedly. "No, I don't remember John Harrison," he said, amused. "He was a little before my time."

"Almost before mine as well," Ridoux went on,

"but I do recall seeing him in his last years. I was only a teenager then, but I spoke to him, telling him of my ambition to become an actor. He encouraged me. But he was a great eccentric, all right."

"He must have been very interesting," Frank said, going back to his work. He realized that the more Ridoux talked, the more the old man's pain was forgotten.

"Very interesting and very eccentric. Did you know that he refused to have any of Shakespeare's tragedies presented on the opera house stage? Oh, he allowed the Bard's comedies to be acted, but never Romeo and Juliet, Othello, Macbeth, Hamlet, King Lear, Julius—"

At that point, Frank found he could push the cinderblock outward. "I think we've got it!" he shouted. He shoved with all of his strength and the building block fell into the back alley. Frank found himself staring into the startled face of a police officer!

In a short time, the policeman had smashed an opening in the wall with a sledgehammer that was large enough for people to enter. Fenton Hardy was the first to leap through to the secret room. He grasped his oldest son in his arms. "Are you all right, Frank?"

Frank grinned. "Just a little bruised, Dad. But Mr. Ridoux is badly hurt. He broke his leg."

The ex-ghost was becoming hysterical. He was

giggling and quoting lines from Shakespeare. Chief Collig, who had come in right behind Mr. Hardy, gave an order, and two officers went for a stretcher. "We have an ambulance outside," he said. "He'll be in the hospital in ten minutes."

The officers did their work efficiently, and Ridoux was whisked into the alley. A moment later, the ambulance's siren was fading down Main Street.

By this time, Joe, Chet, and Mr. Prito had arrived. Chief Collig told them what had happened and added, "I hope that all of you will keep quiet about this room. We're going to wall up the opening so it will look as if it was never disturbed. And mum's the word on Ridoux. We'll keep him closely guarded in the hospital and incognito until we find out exactly what is going on." He turned to Frank. "Now, if you don't mind, I'd like to get a statement from you. I know you've been through a harrowing experience, but I want to learn exactly what happened while it is still fresh in your mind."

"I'll be glad to, Chief," Frank said.

"If you don't need these two any more," Mr. Hardy indicated Joe and Chet, "I think I'll take them home to bed. Then I'll come back for Frank."

"Never mind, Dad," Frank said. "I'll drive the car home."

Before leaving, Joe gave Chief Collig the threatening note to Zandro, the note he found in the car, and the remains of the fake bomb.

"Thanks," said the police chief. "We'll check them out in the morning. I'll be in touch."

Frank told his story quickly into a portable tape recorder. However, Chief Collig asked him to repeat certain answers and to add details so that he was sure he understood.

At last, Frank was free to go. He drove carefully through the Bayport streets. They were deserted at this late hour, but he was aware that his experience of the last few hours had made his reactions slower than usual and extra caution was necessary.

He passed the mysterious black car, which was parked where the occupants could have an unobstructed view of the Hardy residence. There were two men in the front seat of the automobile and one in the back. They did not glance in his direction, but he was certain they knew who was turning into the Hardy driveway.

After making sure the garage doors were securely locked, Frank started towards the rear of the house where he could temporarily turn off the alarm system with a key as he entered. He was moving so swiftly that he almost fell over a shadowy figure trying to peer into a kitchen window!

The stranger tried to run, but Frank grabbed him. There was a brief struggle in which the pair fell off the back porch into the bushes. The trespasser finally shouted, "Okay, okay, that's enough. I give up! I give up!"

Frank shoved the man up against the house. "Talk," he snapped.

"My name is Peter Wilkinson," the intruder said breathlessly. "I'm a reporter for the *New York Gazette*. If you don't believe it, you can check my credentials in my inside coat pocket." He paused, panting. "Kid, you pack a good wallop."

Frank ignored the compliment. "Tell me why you're here and why you've been spying on us."

"Aw, you know why."

"If I did, I wouldn't be asking you."

"Anything to humor you then," Wilkinson said. "I got wind that something really big is about to happen here in Bayport that involved the Hardys and the—"

He never had the opportunity to complete his sentence. The two were hurled to the ground as three men rushed around the corner of the house and attacked them. They were unceremoniously yanked to their feet just as the kitchen lights went on and the back door opened. Fenton Hardy, dressed in his bathrobe, peered out. "What's going on, Donovan?" he asked one of the men.

"We caught your son and this guy talking." Donovan jerked a thumb at Wilkinson. "He was about to spill the beans."

Mr. Hardy held up a warning hand. "All right, bring them in." He and the reporter exchanged hard stares. "Good work, Donovan," the detective said. "Would you please take him upstairs to my office. I'll question him later."

When the three men and Wilkinson had gone, Frank said, "Those were the guys in the black car?"

Fenton Hardy nodded soberly. "But don't ask me any more. I want you to know, though, I'm very grateful that you caught this pest." He grinned at his son. "You've had some night."

Frank smiled back. "You, too."

"And mine's not quite over," his father said ruefully. "But you certainly deserve some sleep. You look pretty tired."

Joe was awake and had the light on when Frank arrived in their bedroom. "What's up?" Joe asked. "I heard this noise and was going down to investigate when I met Dad. He told me to come back in here."

Frank quickly briefed his brother on his capture, then looked at Chet who was lying peacefully in the rollaway bed.

"He slept right through all that noise?" Frank asked.

"You know Chet," Joe said. "He'd sleep right through an earthquake."

Chet, though was the first to wake. When the boys opened their eyes to bright sun streaming through the windows, their friend was sitting on the rollaway bed, observing them gloomily.

"I thought you'd be out all day," he grumbled.

Frank squinted at the clock on his bureau. "It's only eight o'clock and none of us got in until four!"

"It's easy to see you weren't brought up on a farm. It doesn't matter what time we go to sleep; we're out of bed at sunup. Why, I would have had my breakfast over an hour ago!"

Frank laughed, knowing full well that Chet at times had slept into the afternoon. "I bet breakfast is what you really had in mind," he said, throwing a pillow at his friend.

Chet ducked. "Now that you've brought it up, when do we eat?"

"I suppose we'll never get any peace until he's fed," Joe said, rising. "Get dressed, farmboy, and we'll go downstairs and see how good you are at making bacon and eggs."

"Fine hospitality," Chet cried in mock indignation, "inviting someone to stay over and then forcing him to cook or starve."

"It's a tough world, Chet," Joe said, hitting him with another pillow.

They were dressing when they heard loud voices coming from the next room where the two guests from Washington were staying.

"I say we ought to tell headquarters today that this operation should be scrubbed, Doctor!" Jones stormed.

"Nonsense!" the other retorted. "Just because

89

this Wilkinson fellow has learned something—"

"Something? A lot!"

"All right, then, a lot. But he's caught, isn't he? He'll be silenced until afterwards."

"But how do we know how many more know? He may have told his girlfriend or his mother. Too much has leaked out already, I tell you."

"I am in command of this operation," Smith said, "and I will resist any delay. It would be much too dangerous. If we start all over again, it would take many weeks to arrange everything. Don't you understand that we are running out of time? No, he is coming from Washington on Sunday and that is that!"

10 A Ruthless Man

The men's voices trailed off, and the Hardys and Chet looked at each other. What operation were they talking about? Who was coming from Washington on Sunday?

Frank broke the silence. "Let's forget we heard all that and go downstairs."

On their way, they passed the open study door. Fenton Hardy was sitting at his desk, speaking into the telephone. "I tell you this is an urgent call. No, I want to speak to Mr. Girkel, the publisher. No, I cannot tell you what this is about. I repeat, this is Fenton Hardy and I am calling on behalf of the U.S. Government!"

He glanced up and saw the boys looking at him

curiously. The detective made a gesture to Donovan, who was sitting next to the desk. The man rose and approached the door. They heard their father say, "Mr. Girkel? This is a matter of utmost urgency and official secrecy. Last night—"

Then the door closed and his words were cut off.

Peter Wilkinson sat in the downstairs hall. His hands were clasped and he was staring at the floor, the picture of dejection. He looked up and scowled at Frank. "I hope you're satisfied," he said accusingly. "I'm sitting on one of the biggest stories of the year and I can't print a word of it. It's all your fault. Why did you have to butt in?"

Frank looked at him in amazement. "*My* fault? Butt in? You were the one who was sneaking around!"

The reporter dismissed this point with a wave. "Here the press—"

At that moment, two of the men from the black car appeared from the kitchen. "That's enough now," one said sharply. "Only fifteen minutes until your train leaves." They took Wilkinson's arms and propelled him out to their limousine.

Frank looked after the journalist, shaking his head. "A strange man. I'm glad to be rid of him, even though I don't know what this is all about."

Chet did cook the eggs and fry the bacon, although the boys helped him. Fenton came in as they were drinking cocoa. The four sat at the table, discussing the events at both theaters. Frank and Chet were spellbound when Joe told of the written threats that Zandro had been receiving and the fake bomb in the car. In all the excitement of the night, Joe had not had an opportunity to relate his adventures.

"But why would anyone want to hurt Zandro?" asked Chet. "From what you've told me, he doesn't seem like a nice person, especially to other magicians, but he did put this show together."

"There's Manuel, of course," Frank pointed out. "He hates Zandro. He's told everyone that."

"Enough to kill him?" Chet inquired.

"Maybe. Who can tell?" Frank remarked.

"Chet's got a point, though," Joe broke in. "If Manuel does plan to kill Zandro, why now? Why not wait until after the show? And why make himself the most obvious suspect? It doesn't make any sense."

"Hate seldom makes sense," Fenton Hardy put in. "Angry people often act without thinking of the consequences. I have some other news for you. Mr. Prito, as he said he would, has stopped work on the theater. He's padlocked all the doors and put boards over the windows. He realizes that Ridoux did not act alone and he won't send his crew back until he is sure that all danger is past. So none of you has to spend the night in the opera house and, Frank, you can go back to the magician tournament."

"What about Chet, Dad?" Joe asked, seeing his friend's fallen face. "Couldn't he help us at the Palace?"

"Would you like to, Chet?" the detective asked.

Chet's smile was wide. "Would I? I'm crazy about magicians. That would be really interesting. And I'll do a good job, really I will. To tell you the truth, Mr. Hardy, I wasn't too wild about that opera house job. You may not have noticed it, but I was kind of scared."

Joe hid a smile, recalling how Chet had crashed into him while running from the theater after Frank had disappeared. "I never noticed it at all," he said soberly.

"But working at the Palace, that would be different. I'm sure I'll be a great help."

Fenton Hardy smiled. "I'm certain you will. The more hands, the better."

The phone on the wall rang. Frank, who was going to the range for more cocoa, picked it up. "Hardy residence."

"Frank, I've got my handwriting expert at headquarters," Chief Collig said over the phone. "When can you and Joe get here?"

"Is half an hour all right?"

"Fine. See you then."

"The chief is moving fast," Fenton Hardy said when Frank relayed the conversation. "I hope he comes up with some definite clues." He rose.

94

"Well, back to work for me. I'll be glad when this job I'm on is over in a few days and we all can get back to normal."

The boys were inwardly amused; their father's life was far from normal at any time. Mr. Hardy stopped at the door, his face serious. "I know you always take the best of precautions, but, please, be very, very careful. This Palace job started out as a simple routine, just keeping a group of temperamental hotheads apart, but it's become dangerous. Those threatening notes and the fake bomb—the person who was responsible for them is not fooling around. He means business!"

"We'll be careful, Dad," Frank promised and the others nodded their heads.

"Frank, Joe, and Chet, meet Sergeant Kowsky," Chief Collig said. "What he doesn't know about handwriting isn't worth knowing."

Kowsky was a small, energetic officer with a bright smile. "I'm glad to meet you. I've heard a lot about you Hardys, of course."

"Thank you," Frank said.

"And I'm glad to meet you, too, Chet," the sergeant added, pumping the youth's hand vigorously. "Now down to work." He laid the two notes out on the table. "This is fascinating, truly fascinating. In all my years of work, I've never run into anything as interesting."

"But what can you tell them, Stan?" the chief asked impatiently.

"First, the handwriting is a very clever disguise. Second, it is so clever that it is almost impossible to learn much about the person who wrote them."

"Now that's a big help," Joe said, disappointed.

Kowsky held up his hand. "But I can tell you a little bit. The way the "t"s and "y"s fall—you see how they sweep up and down—indicate an egotistical mind, one that might stop at nothing to achieve a goal, one that might be on the edge of insanity. Such a person is ruthless and should be approached with extreme caution."

There was a moment of silence, then Chet whistled. "Wow!"

The sergeant picked up the two papers. "I'll put these back in the files." He shook hands with the youths. "It's been a great pleasure meeting you. I'm sorry I can't tell you more."

After the sergeant had left, Chief Collig said, "I'm afraid I can't be of more help for the moment. We checked the fake bomb for fingerprints, but came up negative. As you might have guessed, the person who handled it probably wore gloves. Furthermore, we traced the device to a Chicago firm that made magicians' equipment. Unfortunately, the company went out of business two years ago and all sales receipts were destroyed."

"A real dead end," Frank concluded. "Thanks

anyhow, Chief. Did you hear anything about Mr. Ridoux?"

The police officer chuckled as he rose. "He's a tough old bird. The break was clean and not too complicated. Of course, at his age, healing could be difficult, but the doctors believe his recovery will be complete. His mind seems to be clearing and his appetite is good. He says he wants to visit Tony Prito to apologize, but we won't let him do that since we don't want to have any holes in the curtain of secrecy we've put up."

He walked them to the door. "I don't know what I can say, except to warn you to be careful."

"Dad gave us a lecture on that this morning." Joe grinned.

"Well, what he said goes double for me!"

The ride back to the Hardy home was very quiet, each youth lost in his own thoughts. They had an uneasy feeling that danger lay ahead.

The black car was once more parked in its usual spot. In front of the house was another vehicle, an official government automobile bearing the legend U.S. NAVY on its door.

Fenton Hardy and a naval officer were speaking in the hall as the boys entered. "The publisher promised that he'll keep the reporter under wraps and—" Fenton was saying, but broke off abruptly when he saw his sons.

11　Mad Manuel

"Captain Svensen, I would like to introduce my sons," Fenton Hardy said. "This is Joe and behind him is Frank."

The officer grinned. "One blond and one with dark hair. Good variety, Fenton."

"And this is Chet Morton, one of their friends."

Svensen shook hands with all three youths. Frank realized this was the commander of the Bayport Naval Base, a military installation five miles outside the city. It was used as a submarine training school and also had a large hospital, one of the best in the country.

"Are you keeping yourselves busy this summer?" the captain asked. "When I was your age, summers used to drive me crazy. It was fun at first, but a couple of weeks after school closed, boredom would set in. I worked in my dad's store, but I was always wishing to do something else."

Frank thought of the events of the last couple of days—broken legs, a ghost, excitable magicians with knives, threatening letters, secret panels and rooms, a fake bomb. "Oh, we manage to keep busy, sir," he said with a serious expression on his face.

"The three of them are on security duty at the Palace while the magician tournament is going on," the detective said.

"That's great!" the captain exclaimed. "It must be a lot of fun."

"Yes, sir, it has been a lot of fun," Joe said with a straight face.

"Say, I might see you three tonight. One hundred of our personnel have been invited by one of the participants, a Mr. Handro, Bando, or something like that."

"Zandro?" Frank asked.

"That's the name. I've heard that he's pretty good."

"Very good, sir," Joe said. "Probably the best."

"Well, it was a very nice thing for him to do," said the captain. He turned to Fenton Hardy. "I have to get back. Thanks for the coffee. All is prepared for Sunday. It's an awesome responsibility, but my people are up to it." He shook hands, smiled pleasantly at the youths, and left.

When Frank, Joe, and Chet arrived at the theater at six o'clock they found Mr. Heifitz beside himself in rage. "That Zandro! How dare he do this to me?"

Frank had a sinking feeling. "He is going to show up tonight, isn't he? Those threatening letters didn't scare him off? I mean, there's a lot of sailors coming this evening at his invitation and—"

"Oh, yes, he'll be here," the theater manager snapped, "to bask in all his glory and to receive the gratitude of the navy. That's the kind of thing that's bread and butter to him. But does he think of me? Never! Here he sends Hortell, practically at the last minute, to demand a hundred seats to be set aside for his naval guests. I wouldn't mind if he had done this three days ago, but now! He realizes full well that this sort of thing is not easily arranged. I've got to put them in all sections of the theater because it's impossible at this point to seat them together. I have to—"

Suddenly his attitude changed and he broke out in a bright smile. "I'm a dolt! I've seen the day when I would have been grateful to get twenty more people into the house. Now I'm infuriated because it is going to be packed. Zandro could have had more consideration but at least he did pay full price for all the sailors."

"Let's hope the show goes all right tonight," Chet said.

Mr. Heifitz's joy vanished as quickly as it had come. "Oh, my, let's hope so. We've had all this trouble. The police were around to question me about it. I feel that more of this is going to happen."

The three youths left the theater manager wringing his hands. "He's a man of many moods," Joe observed as they proceeded backstage.

Frank laughed. "And they seem to come and go as fast as turning a light on and off."

Mr. Heifitz's fears concerning the show were unfounded, however. It turned out to be the best performance so far. The four magicians were at the top of their form. Frank, Joe, and Chet gasped at the brilliant rendering of illusions, each one seeming better than the last. It was obvious, though, that Zandro and Manuel were superior to their competitors, and no one protested when they were selected for the finals on the following evening. Even the two losers vigorously applauded the decision.

As the audience was filing out, the young detectives came from their positions backstage to greet Captain Svensen. "Wasn't the show wonderful?" the officer exclaimed enthusiastically. "I'm sure the men and women from our base would agree. I don't want to disturb him now, but would you please pass our thanks to Zandro?"

"We'll be happy to, sir," Frank said.

In back of the curtain, though, the scene was far from peaceful. When the Hardys and Chet returned, they found Zandro and Manuel screaming at each other, their noses almost touching. Happy Hortell and Mr. Heifitz stood to one side, looking very worried.

"You pompous elephant!" Manuel called his arch rival. "Taking ten curtain calls when five would have been enough. You milked that audience for all you could."

"They wanted me," the heavyset magician snarled, "which is more than can be said for you, judging by the anemic applause you received more out of pity than admiration."

Manuel was livid with rage. "I shall make you pay for those words. Just wait, just you wait!"

Zandro looked down at his enemy and sneered, "What will you do? Send me more of your threatening notes? Pull another knife?"

Manuel's face turned white. "I never had a knife and you know it. And what's all this about threatening notes?"

"Zandro has been receiving them under his door," Joe explained.

"And I'm the chief suspect, eh? Another one of his sly tricks." Manuel glared at Zandro with so much hate that Joe and Frank moved near instinctively to prevent violence. "I shall defeat you in the only arena I know—the stage," Manuel continued.

"Tomorrow night I shall crush your massive egotism under my heel before hundreds of people. For the first time, you shall know humiliation, Zandro."

There was a moment of tense silence, then it was broken by a roar of laughter from Zandro. "Get away from me, little man," he bellowed.

"Tomorrow night," Manuel hissed and walked towards his dressing room.

Nothing more happened. An hour later, the youths stood just outside the front entrance as Mr. Heifitz locked the door. "One more night," the theater manager said. "This whole thing has taken ten years out of my life. I must really thank you. I am positive that much worse would have happened if you had not been here."

"It's going to be all right tomorrow, too, Mr. Heifitz," Joe said. "You'll see."

"I only hope you're right," the manager said. "But I do have this terrible premonition. Good night."

Frank and Joe were light sleepers and usually rose early. But even Chet, who was staying with the Hardys for the duration of their assignment, was startled out of his dreams the next morning because a steady hum of conversation was coming from the first floor.

When the boys went down, they found the hallway packed with people. They recognized Randolph Hopple, the head of the local FBI office and their father's good friend. He was talking to the men who had kept watch in the black limousine.

Captain Svensen saw the youths and walked up to them. "When I got into my office this morning, I found a message that Zandro had phoned late last night to offer a free show for the children in our hospital." He beamed.

"Hey, that's real nice," Chet said.

"It certainly is. I phoned his hotel and talked to a Mr. Hortell. Zandro is coming to the hospital tomorrow morning. Well, we all have to be going now. When you see him tonight, please give Zandro my thanks again. The kids are going to be tickled."

The crowd began to move through the door, almost knocking over a messenger carrying two boxes. He managed to squeeze himself in. "Mrs. Fenton Hardy, Miss Gertrude Hardy?" he asked.

Mr. Smith, who was addressed as Dr. Smith by someone, hurried forward. "Those are ours, I think." He signed for them and gave the messenger a tip. "Jones, our gifts are here."

Jones, who was going through the door, returned. "Good, they came early."

Smith smiled at Mrs. Hardy and Aunt Gertrude as he extended the long, thin boxes. "These are peace offerings from Mr. Jones and myself. We know that we have been terrible nuisances, being more intruders than guests, having our meals served in our rooms. Believe me, all of it was very necessary, as I know you will learn one day. In the meantime, please accept these gifts, which are small indeed compared to your wonderful hospitality."

The women opened the boxes. Inside of each were a dozen long-stemmed roses. The only difference was that Mrs. Hardy received red roses while Aunt Gertrude's were white.

"Thank you so much," Mrs. Hardy said, and Aunt Gertrude grunted her gratitude. The two men made small bows and disappeared through the door.

"Huh," Aunt Gertrude sniffed. "The garden is full of roses and they give us more. Some gift."

"Oh, but these are different," her sister-in-law cried.

Aunt Gertrude relented a little as she gazed at her flowers. "Well, maybe. But I don't think I'll ever grow to like that Smith fellow. Oily smile."

"You may not have to bother with them any more, since they've left. You may never see them again."

"Which is not too soon for me," Aunt Gertrude said with finality.

Fenton Hardy came into the hallway from outside. "Well, they're off. Will all of you please come into my study for a few minutes?"

When everyone was seated, he closed the door and sat at his desk. "I know the last few days have been a strain with Jones and Smith as our boarders and being watched by the men in the black car night and day. That phase is now over and you won't be disturbed further." He paused. "I'm going to be away for a few days. I can't tell you where I will be. I'll try to call now and then, but I'll be very busy. So if you don't hear from me often, don't get worried."

The family took this calmly. After all, Fenton Hardy had been away before. They saw him to the door and waved as he drove away. He had no sooner gone when another car pulled up.

"Now who's this?" Aunt Gertrude said, annoyed.

"It's Manuel the Magnificent," Joe exclaimed in surprise.

"Manuel who?" Mrs. Hardy asked.

"The Magnificent," Frank said.

"He calls himself that? He certainly doesn't think much of himself, does he?" Aunt Gertrude muttered before she and Mrs. Hardy disappeared into the house to arrange the roses.

"Here comes trouble," Chet muttered.

"He doesn't look like he's on the warpath," Joe observed.

"I would like to speak with you, please," the magician said when he reached them.

Frank nodded. "Certainly. I think our laboratory would be the most private place." He led the way to the room above the garage.

Manuel looked around the laboratory with awe. "You are more than amateurs in science, I can see that."

"We enjoy experiments," Joe said and indicated a small couch. "Won't you sit down?"

Manuel settled back before speaking. "I will not waste my words. I know you suspect me of the things that have happened at the Palace this week. I don't know what I can do to convince you that I am innocent, but I plead with you to keep an open mind. I do not carry knives, I do not write threatening letters, I do not smash my competitors' equipment."

"We always keep an open mind," Frank said.

Manuel looked from one boy to the other and noticed the skepticism on their faces. He rose with a sudden bound. "I can see that this is useless. You believe that scoundrel, Zandro, in everything he says and does. You don't even see how jealous he is of me. He is a great magician, I admit that, but he is also an egomaniac and dangerous. But I might as well be talking to a stone wall. That madman has you hypnotized!"

With that parting remark, Manuel was gone. They watched him cross the lawn towards his car.

"He sure is angry," Joe said. "He wouldn't believe we have open minds."

"I wonder if we do," Frank said slowly.

12 Sandbag Scare

While Frank and Chet kept a sharp lookout for danger backstage, Joe went to see Mr. Heifitz in the box office.

"I'm glad you're here," the theater manager greeted him. "Would you give me a hand, Joe? Mrs. Winters, who usually helps me, has the flu and can't come. It'll only be for a couple of hours."

Joe readily agreed. Selling tickets was a relief from the security watch. Furthermore, only two people were needed backstage for the show.

The performance was a sellout. People started lining up for tickets at six o'clock. By seven-thirty, there was not a seat to be had. The box office had to be kept open, though, for those who had reserved tickets by phone.

Mr. Heifitz was alternately deliriously happy or in the deepest gloom. One minute, he foresaw the most dire consequences for the evening's performance; the next minute he marveled that the week's receipts had broken the theater's record and said he was sure tonight would be an artistic triumph.

At eight-thirty sharp, the footlights dimmed. The chief judge stepped before the curtain to explain the reason for the contest, and how fourteen illusionists had been eliminated. "Now only Zandro and Manuel remain to battle upon this venerable stage. May the best magician win!"

There was loud cheering. After clearing his throat, the chief judge announced, "The finalists have flipped a coin backstage to determine their positions on tonight's program. That toss was won by Manuel, who chose to be last. Therefore, ladies and gentlemen, it is my pleasure to introduce the great Zandro!"

There was tumultuous applause, and Zandro's most ardent supporters whistled and stamped their feet when the curtain opened. The magician appeared at the side of the stage, bowed, and then started to march across to a table in the center.

There was a sudden shout, "Zandro, look out!"

The man jumped backwards. A gray object fell to the stage with a thud.

Someone in the front row screamed, "It's a body!" For a moment, it looked as if the audience

might panic, which would have been a disaster in the packed theater. But with a spirit that surprised Frank and Joe, Mr. Heifitz walked upon the stage and raised his hands for silence. There was something about the small man that commanded attention and the audience became quiet.

"It's not a body," he informed the people before him, "but a bag of sand used as one of the weights to raise and lower the curtain. Somehow it fell, for which the management of this theater deeply apologizes. Now we must beg your indulgence as we lower the curtain for a few minutes. Please bear with us as we make repairs."

He snapped his fingers and the curtain came down. When it had reached the floor, he turned around and rushed to Zandro. The Hardys, Chet, and Happy Hortell ran in from the wings.

"Are you all right?" Mr. Heifitz asked anxiously, peering into the magician's face. Zandro was shaking violently, his eyes transfixed on the sandbag. "That might have killed me," he managed to croak.

"That Manuel did it!" Happy Hortell shouted. "I saw him up on the balcony. He must have cut the rope."

"What is this? What am I accused of this time?" The little magician strode upon the stage.

"A sandbag fell and narrowly missed Zandro," Frank explained.

111

"Another one of his hallucinations," Manuel sneered.

"Look at Zandro. Does he appear to be hallucinating?" Joe snapped angrily. "Do you think he conjured up that sandbag by magic?" He pointed to the gray object on the stage.

It was Manuel's turn to look ashen. He held out his hands helplessly. "But I had nothing to do with this, believe me!" he pleaded.

"He was up on that balcony," Hortell snarled. "I saw him!"

Frank scratched his head. "Manuel's word against Happy's. That seems like a stand-off. Chet, your post was near the balcony. What did you see?"

The stocky youth looked ashamed. "To tell the truth, I wasn't there all the time. I came forward for a few seconds to take a peek at that judge while he was speaking. I wasn't gone long. I didn't see Manuel go *up* the balcony ladder. I only saw him when he came *down*."

"Down!" Joe and Frank exclaimed together.

"It's true, I was up there," the magician admitted. "I had come out of my dressing room when I saw a shadowy figure go up the ladder. I couldn't see any of you fellows so I decided to follow and see what this person was up to."

"And did you notice anyone?" Frank asked.

The little magician looked helpless as he began to

realize how guilty he appeared. "No one. I hadn't been up there long, though, when I heard all this yelling. I came down to investigate."

"That's when I caught him," Chet said, "when he came down the ladder after the yelling started, before Mr. Heifitz calmed everyone."

"What about the other person?" Joe asked. "Did you see him, too?"

Chet shook his head. "But then I came forward to hear what Mr. Heifitz was saying."

"Gentlemen, let's iron this out later," Mr. Heifitz said, his hands fluttering nervously. "It's time to begin again if you've had enough time to rest, Zandro."

Zandro looked at him with wild eyes. "Go on? You don't believe for one instant that I am going through with my act. Why, it will be weeks before I'm in top form again."

"But the audience, it's a packed house!" wailed the theater manager. "The show must go on."

"It may go on," said Zandro, "but not with me in it, not over my dead body," and he indicated the sandbag, "which it almost was."

Mr. Heifitz was shocked. "It's the tradition of the theater. Anyway, don't you realize I will have to pay those people back for the cancellation of a show that was your idea in the first place?"

Zandro put his hand on the theater manager's

shoulder. "Do not be concerned, old friend. I guarantee that you will not lose one penny. I will have Happy give you all the money you return tonight. Right now, though, I think I shall go to the dressing room. I feel faint."

Aided by Hortell, Zandro walked towards the wings. A furious Manuel glared after him. "He's done it again! I shall not stay in this theater one more second! I'm leaving!" He turned on his heel and stamped out towards the rear exit.

"I better check to see that he really does leave," Joe said and disappeared after the small magician.

Mr. Heifitz sighed. "I predicted something like this would happen! Now I must go tell the audience." He slipped through the curtain, the murmurs in the building died, and he began, "Ladies and gentlemen, it is my unhappy duty to announce that . . ."

Frank tapped Chet's shoulder. "We better stand guard at Zandro's dressing room."

As they left the stage, they heard groans, hisses, and boos from the audience. "That Mr. Heifitz is really something," Chet said. "Imagine predicting that tonight's show was going to be cancelled!"

Frank smiled grimly. "From what Joe said, he couldn't miss. His predictions ran all the way from doom to joy."

They stopped opposite the dressing-room door.

Joe joined them a minute later. "Manuel went out the exit, all right. What a night!"

"It just started and now the assignment is ended," Chet said in an aggrieved tone. "I was looking forward to seeing the show."

"Maybe we can arrange for you to see another," Frank said.

"What do you mean?"

"Just wait and see."

The door opened and Happy Hortell came out. He looked at the youths and said gruffly, "There's no reason to stick around."

"We have to see you and Zandro leave the theater safely," Frank said. "Then our responsibility is over."

"That's so? Well, it won't be long. I have to zip up to Heifitz's office and give him a check. I'll be right back." Hortell trotted off, leaving the dressing room door ajar.

"Is that the Hardy boys?" came a familiar voice from the dressing room. "Come on in."

The boys entered. Zandro was sitting in a chair, dressed in street clothes.

"How do you feel?" Joe asked.

"Oh, much better now, thanks. But it was a tremendous shock. I was a fool not to take his threats seriously. I am glad, though, that you were around to see it for yourselves."

"It's really very nice of you to give a show for the children at the naval hospital," Frank remarked. "You'll have all this equipment to lug out there?" He indicated several large boxes.

"Yes."

"Then why don't we give you a hand? You'll never get all that in your van."

There was a moment of hesitation, then the magician said jovially, "That's very kind of you. We'll be happy to take your offer of aid. Be here tomorrow at eight in the morning."

When Happy Hortell returned, Zandro told him of the boys' offer of help. Hortell looked surprised and muttered, "We don't need anyone. I can handle all the moving of the equipment."

Zandro fixed steely eyes on his manager. "I believe that we require their assistance, Happy." The other looked sullen, but did not reply.

"Now I believe that we are ready to depart, are we not?" Zandro asked. "The check has been given to Mr. Heifitz? Good. Then we shall see the Hardys and Chet tomorrow."

After leaving, Chet said, "Peter Walker is having a few people over to his house tonight. Why don't we drop in for a little while?"

"Sure, why not?" Frank drove toward the Walker home, which was not far from the airport. "Something bothers me," he said as they went along. "It didn't seem very professional of Zandro to stop the show, and then to reimburse Heifitz for the ticket sales."

Joe nodded. "It was odd. Even though he's a big star and certainly has plenty of money."

"I wouldn't want to do magic tricks after such a close encounter with death!" Chet spoke up. "I mean, you get jittery when something like that happens."

Suddenly, as Frank rounded a turn, he found himself confronting a roadblock. Two police cars were parked on the side, and an officer flashed a light into the Hardys' sports sedan. "You'll have to wait for a few minutes," he told them.

"What's going on?" Joe asked.

"Our orders are that the air terminal and all roads adjacent to it for a distance of a quarter-mile are off limits until we get the word that everything is all clear. I guess some big shot is coming in," the policeman replied.

Frank, Joe, and Chet had an unobstructed view of the airfield. A large plane with an air force insignia on it had just landed. A helicopter stood nearby and people were running between the two craft.

Then the helicopter's door closed and, with a roar, the chopper lifted into the sky. As soon as it had disappeared, the patrol cars' radios crackled,

"All clear at the air terminal. Suspend roadblocks and continue on regular duty."

The officer who had spoken to them pulled the roadblock aside and waved them on.

"Now that was interesting," Chet said, "but what did it all mean?"

Neither Frank nor Joe had an answer.

"I don't think you can get one more carton in," Joe said. It was eight-thirty in the morning. The three boys and Happy Hortell had been packing Zandro's van and the back of their car. "How do you transport all your equipment from city to city when you can only get half of it in your van?"

"Oh, we usually ship it by truck," Zandro said. He looked at the cartons stacked in the foyer of the theater and sighed. "I suppose two trips are in order."

"There's no other way," Frank agreed. "Suppose Chet and I follow the van out to the naval hospital. We could stay there and carry the boxes in, so Happy wouldn't have to spend any more time there than necessary. Joe could stay here and help load when Happy returns."

"A splendid idea!" Zandro cried. "I couldn't think of a better one myself. Don't you think it is a wise course of action, Happy?"

His unsmiling friend shrugged. "Let's go."

118

"Happy doesn't do his name justice," Joe remarked as the van and the Hardys' car drove away.

"He has his moods," Zandro said. "This is one of his despondent ones. But he'll be 'Happy' soon again, I assure you. Why do we stand here on the sidewalk in all this heat? Let's go back to the dressing room where we can rest and be cool."

They marched through the foyer, passing the box office where Mr. Heifitz was working on a sheet of figures. Zandro waved cheerily at him, but the theater manager returned only a cursory nod.

Zandro opened the dressing-room door and turned on the lights and air conditioner. "Oh, yes, this will be much better. Sit over there, Joe, in that comfortable chair. Don't mind me if I pace up and down. I feel exhilarated today, too exhilarated to sit still."

"I thought you would be recovering from the shock of last night," Joe said.

Zandro dismissed his mishap on the stage with a wave of his hand. "My philosophy is to forget yesterday, live for today, and plan for tomorrow. And today is a wonderful day. I feel excited because something wonderful is going to happen. I'm psychic, you know."

"What's going to happen?" Frank asked.

The magician chuckled. "I like to keep my visions secret until after they occur."

119

Joe, who did not believe in psychic phenomena, was tired of the conversation and changed the subject. "Aren't you disappointed about how the week turned out?"

"Oh, of course, I am. But I can find consolation because that charlatan Manuel was exposed in all his viciousness."

"If you're so sure he did all this, why don't you file a complaint with the police and have him arrested?" Joe questioned.

"Never mind that. He's already suffering his just punishment. He will not be able to step on many stages after what he tried to do gets around in the trade. Anyway, no one actually saw him cut the rope and release the sandbag. It wouldn't stand up in a court of law."

Zandro continued to pace, which made Joe nervous.

"Anyway, it was a week of great nostalgia," Zandro continued. "As you know, I have a soft spot in my heart for Bayport. What memories I have of playing the Palace and the opera house!" He laughed. "Yes, I'm even fond of the good old ghost, Alebert Cavendish."

"The opera house certainly is an interesting place," Joe said. "It must have some history. My brother told me that he heard that around 1900, there was a theater manager named John Harrison who had something against playing Shakespeare's tragedies. He wouldn't let them be performed. Say, he must have been the manager when Cavendish was killed."

Zandro, who had been walking behind Joe's chair, stopped. Joe looked up at that moment into the large make-up mirror and saw the reflection of the magician. The man was glaring down at Joe with a look of pure hate. Then, realizing that Joe was staring at him, his expression instantly changed back to jovial benevolence.

The incident was enough to jolt Joe into a sudden realization. According to what Zandro had told them earlier, Cavendish, whose ghost the magician supposedly encountered in the dressing room, had played Hamlet's father. Yet, during Harrison's reign as the manager of the theater, Shakespeare's tragedies were not allowed to be performed!

Zandro was a liar!

13 Joe's Mistake

The revelation must have shown in Joe's face in the mirror. Before he could act, the edge of Zandro's hand slammed down on the back of the youth's neck, and he sank into unconsciousness.

He had no idea how long he was out, but it must have been more than an hour. He opened his eyes and groggily saw Happy Hortell entering the room.

"What's going on?" Hortell asked, staring down at Joe.

"Close the door, you fool!" hissed Zandro. Hortell obeyed immediately. "The boy stumbled on to the ghost trick. He knows it was a fake."

Joe tried to protest, but found his mouth was gagged.

"Go out to the stage and get some rope. There's always a length or two lying around," ordered Zandro.

When Hortell had left, Joe's hands started up to his mouth to tear the gag off.

"Don't try that," Zandro said softly. "I would have to hit you again and I'm afraid I might kill you by accident. You see, when I was younger, I was a judo expert."

Joe saw the menace in the man's eyes and let his hands drop.

"That's better." Zandro shook his head. "It truly grieves me to treat you like this, but you did guess our secret, part of it, at least. Sometimes—I must admit—I am too clever for my own good. We should have checked deeper into the history of the opera house. I didn't know that John Harrison barred Shakespeare's tragedies when I made up the ghost story."

Hortell re-entered, carrying about six feet of rope.

"Good work, Happy! We'll tie him up." In a moment, they had Joe bound. "Now let's carry him over to that old trunk behind the screen."

They lowered him into it. "Did you guess that Ridoux was the ghost?" Zandro asked. "But, of course, you must have known. Frank fell down the stairs to the secret room where Ridoux was trapped.

Somehow, they both got out. I suppose Ridoux is in the hospital. Happy and I were stunned when Frank came into the theater tonight, but we soon guessed that we weren't your prime suspects."

He laughed, and Joe saw sparks of insanity dancing in the magician's eyes.

"I almost gave poor Happy a heart attack when I went along with Frank's suggestion that you help us here this morning. Happy was against the whole idea, of course, but I am the leader and I make the decisions. I convinced him that it was better to have you three where we could keep an eye on you."

"We're wasting time," Hortell growled behind him.

"So we are," Zandro said. "Well, good-bye, Joe. If I remember, I'll tell the police later where you are." He smiled and repeated, "If I remember."

The lid came down and there was the click of a lock. Joe was alone in darkness.

Chet and Frank were sitting on a bench in front of the hospital when Zandro and Hortell drove up.

"We put the equipment in a room next to the children's ward," Frank said.

"Splendid, splendid," Zandro said as he emerged from the van. "It will be easy working from there. Now if you two could help Happy take the rest of our paraphernalia inside, I would be most grateful." He noticed Frank looking around for his brother and

124

added, "Joe received a phone call from Jonathan Ridoux. The old man wanted to see him right away."

"Oh, I guess that's pretty important then," Frank said, smiling. "Joe will get in touch with me later. Don't try to lift that all by yourself, Chet. Let me get on the other side."

Frank's easy tone disguised a deep anxiety and growing suspicion. If Ridoux had indeed contacted Joe, the younger Hardy would not have divulged this information to anyone except in an emergency. What was Zandro up to? Frank wondered, but for the time being, he decided to play along.

Very close to the children's ward was a long corridor guarded by three marines. Chet and Frank cast curious glances at the sentries standing stiffly at attention, but Zandro and Hortell walked by to the children's ward, seemingly oblivious.

"Hey, isn't that your father?" Chet asked when the two went out for the last of the boxes. Indeed Fenton Hardy was talking to two men in the center of the guarded corridor. When he saw Frank and Chet, he looked startled. Then he smiled and waved before hurrying away in the opposite direction.

"This last one is pretty heavy," Chet complained as they carried in a small wooden crate. "I wonder why it's marked with an X."

"Got me," Frank grunted.

When Happy Hortell saw the crate, he became nervous. "I thought that was already in," he said. "Be careful, don't drop it. Put it in that room next to the children's ward."

Zandro was in the room, fixing his top hat at a rakish angle. "How does this look? I have no mirror to see myself."

"It looks fine," Chet said.

"I'm trying to present a slightly different image to the children than I do to the adults. They are really two different types of audiences and cannot be handled in the same manner. Be careful of that crate, will you? It's most important to my act. Ah, Happy, there you are. How do I look?"

"Like the magician's magician," Hortell said.

"Then on with the show! Are you ready, gentlemen?"

"I'll stay in here for a moment and straighten out all these boxes," Chet offered. Frank looked up in surprise, as Chet had never been eager to volunteer for extra work, but then he shrugged and followed the magician.

They entered the children's ward from another door in the small room. Captain Svensen was already there.

"Now girls and boys, we have a real treat for you this morning," the naval officer announced. "Zandro, the world's greatest magician, has come here especially to entertain you. I have seen many of his tricks and I know you're going to be as amazed as I was. I only wish I could stay and watch them again, but I've got duty elsewhere. So let's all give Zandro a great big hand!"

The children in the beds and wheelchairs clapped vigorously. Captain Svensen shook hands with Zandro and left.

The magician turned towards the children. "Girls and boys, thank you so much for inviting me and my friends here today. I would like to give you something to show my appreciation."

He waved his hands in the air and suddenly a bouquet of flowers appeared in them. The children gasped at the suddenness of the trick.

"But perhaps you don't appreciate flowers." He put the flowers into a vase on a small table that Hortell placed near him. "Maybe you would like—" he waved his hands in the air again—"a rabbit!" And there was one, wriggling and trembling. Zandro soothed the animal and put it into a cage on the table. "There may be some of you who prefer—" the hands went up again—"a lovely bird!" And Zandro was holding a dove. It flew up and around the ward until the magician whistled. Then the dove flew back into his hands. When they had recovered from their amazement, the children clapped and cheered.

Frank had thought Zandro had been brilliant during his Palace shows, but it was obvious that the star was surpassing his usual standards of excellence this morning. He found coins behind children's ears, took eight eggs out of his mouth, balanced three billiard balls on top of his head, and did a variety of dazzling tricks, each one more astonishing then the last.

There was only one interruption. In the middle of a trick, the door to the hall opened and the man that the boys knew as Smith walked in. He was wearing a white coat, which didn't surprise Frank since he knew the Hardys' former guest was a doctor.

Smith walked several steps into the room, seemingly unaware of where he was. All eyes were glued on him, and Zandro stopped his trick when Smith looked up. "Oh," he said in an embarrassed tone. "Excuse me. I opened the wrong door."

He then turned and hurriedly left the room. The children laughed after he had gone, and Zandro held up his hands in a gesture that signified, What else can you expect from some people?

He completed his trick and, once more, raised his hands for silence. "Now I am going to perform the greatest trick of my life. It is one which will truly astound you. But I must ask for your absolute patience. Having patience should not be difficult for you since you are patients, are you not?"

The children laughed at this poor joke. He had them completely under his spell.

"I must step out of the room for a little while," he continued. "While I am gone, I ask that you be very, very quiet. That is most necessary for the successful completion of my trick. You will promise me to be quiet, won't you?"

The children nodded, eager to please this man who had brightened their lives with his magic.

"Good. Come along, Happy." Zandro began to tiptoe towards the door, which made the small patients laugh again.

As Happy passed the young detectives, Chet made a move to follow. Hortell snapped his head around and hissed, "Not you, dummy. You stay here with Hardy."

The men disappeared into the small room that the magician was using for storage and closed the door behind them. Surprisingly, the children remained silent, only looking at each other from time to time and giggling softly.

"He's not very polite, that Hortell, calling me a dummy," Chet whispered.

"No, he isn't," Frank replied. "He seems very tense today."

Chet grinned. "That must be some trick Zandro is going to pull. What do you think gas masks have to do with it?"

"Gas masks?" Frank replied, frowning.

"Well, you remember when I hung back to make the small room neat? The real reason I did that was that it gave me a chance to look over the equipment. I'd like to be a magician some day and I was wondering—"

"What about the gas masks?" Frank interrupted.

"They were in the last crate, the one that Hortell was so nervous about. There were some funny-looking cylinders in there, too."

"Something is fishy, Chet. Come on!" The two hurried towards the door.

No one was in the room next door, but the crate was empty. From the hallway came the sound of hissing. Frank charged out, followed closely by Chet.

They gasped at what they saw. The three marine sentries were lying face down on the floor. In the corridor was a thick cloud, which looked like white smoke, and an acrid gassy odor permeated the air.

Suddenly, two men emerged from the white fog. One, in a flowing black cape, was pushing a gurney with a patient on it. The other ran alongside, holding a cylinder like a rifle. Both wore gas masks.

When the gurney came closer, Frank was able to take a good look at the inert form lying on it with his eyes closed.

He gasped. Although he had never met the patient nor seen him in person, he knew him very well from pictures and television. *The unconscious man on the gurney was the president of the United States!*

14   The Gas Caper

"Get them, Chet," Frank cried. He didn't know what was going on, only that the president was being taken away, apparently without his knowledge, and the Hardy boy did not have to look behind the gas masks to know the identity of the abductors. Their clothes showed only too well that they were Zandro and Happy Hortell!

Frank and Chet immediately sprang into action, but their lunges were not fast enough to halt the getaway. Hortell lifted the cylinder in his hand, touched a button, and a spurt of cloudy gas shot out. Frank dodged to one side, breathing only a whiff, but Chet received a full blast in the face and collapsed.

Frank fell to the floor and rolled away. Zandro

and Hortell dashed towards the hospital's front entrance with their victim. Frank struggled to his feet and started in pursuit of the fleeing kidnappers, but the small amount of gas he had inhaled made him groggy. He staggered through the reception area where startled nurses were still gazing after the gurney. The boy stumbled into the parking lot just in time to see Zandro closing the back doors of the van.

"Stop!" Frank croaked.

The magician gave him an angry glance, then jumped into the driver's seat and started the engine.

Incapacitated as he was, Frank nevertheless managed to reach the rear of the van. With an enormous effort, he pulled open the doors and crawled inside.

The president was lying on a mattress. Sitting next to him with a sinister smile was Happy Hortell. He grabbed Frank; there was a brief struggle in which Frank landed a few good blows, but in the end his weakened condition took its toll. Hortell's fists clipped Frank on the jaw several times, and he fell into unconsciousness.

Joe had borrowed a trick from the great Houdini when Hortell had tied him. He had tensed his muscles as tightly as he could while the rope was being lashed around his arms and legs. He was surprised that his captors had not spotted this ruse, but he supposed their attention was on their evil plans.

When he was certain that they had left the theater and would not return, he began to work his way out of his bonds. The slight slackness of the ropes he achieved by relaxing his muscles enabled him to slowly free himself. He tore the gag from his mouth and took the ropes off his legs.

Then he put his feet against the lid of the trunk and pushed upward with all his strength. But the cover did not budge. He attempted to free himself by kicking at the lid. Again, no success!

He realized that he was in an extremely dangerous situation. He lay still to calmly think of alternatives, a method he had been taught by his father. If I use too much energy in trying to escape, I will quickly exhaust the air and suffocate, he thought. However, I cannot just lie here and hope to be discovered sooner or later. Therefore, I will kick the sides of the trunk at intervals in the hope that someone will hear me.

He counted slowly to 100 and then kicked the trunk fifteen times. He then lay back and counted to 100 again and repeated the kicks. After ten such attempts, his head started to reel. He could feel his strength ebbing. Obviously, he had used up a great deal of the precious oxygen. He counted 97 . . . 98 . . . 99 . . . 100, and then began to kick again.

On the fifth try, his legs fell down, unable to continue, and he started to slip into unconsciousness.

Suddenly, the lid opened and, through a haze caused by his weakness, Joe saw a startled Manuel staring down at him!

Joe slowly rose out of the trunk, aided by Manuel, who eased him into a chair.

"I'm lucky you arrived," Joe said when he had recovered his breath. "Another five minutes and it would have been too late."

"I had to come back to pick up my equipment," Manuel explained. "I heard the pounding, but my first thought was to avoid entering Zandro's room under any circumstances. However, I peeked in and saw that the sound came from the trunk so I decided to investigate. It was fortunate that the lock was loose; otherwise, it would have been most difficult to free you. Who did this to you?"

"Zandro," Joe panted. He looked across at the open trunk that had almost been his coffin. On its side was printed:

RUDOLPH DUVALIER
ZANDRO

Manuel looked puzzled. "But why? I knew the man was out of his mind, but I never thought he was this crazy."

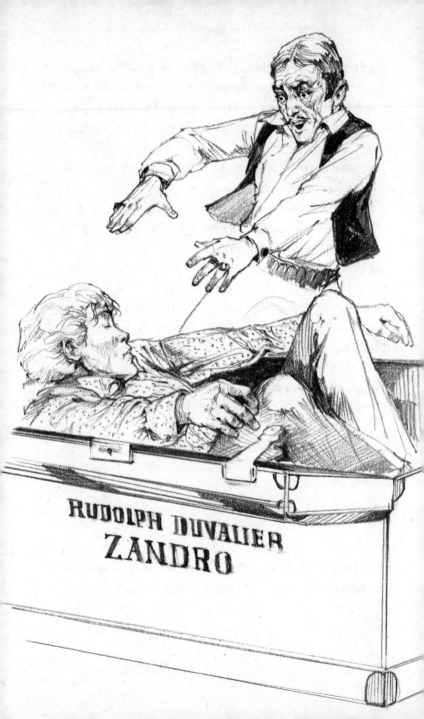

"I found out that he told a lie about the ghost at the opera house. The lie knocked down his whole story."

Manuel was bewildered. "What ghost? What about that old theater? What—"

Joe had completely recovered by this time. "Do you have a car?" he interrupted.

"Yes, outside, but—"

"We've got to get to the naval base right away," Joe urged. "Something strange is taking place out there. I don't know what it is, but you can bet that Zandro is at the bottom of it."

"If Zandro is mixed up in this, then it will be my pleasure to take you to the naval base to foil him."

As they drove towards the military installation, Joe related all that had occurred during the past few days in the opera house.

"That Zandro!" Manuel exclaimed, his hands clenched tightly around the steering wheel. "You see it is as I said. He's been trying to frame me!"

"He's a tricky one, all right," Joe said. He did not point out that what happened at the opera house did not clear Manuel of being a possible suspect in the Palace Theater events. "There's a police car! Stop, will you, please?"

Manuel pulled up behind the patrol car. Two officers sat in it observing traffic on the highway. One of them was Dan Corey, whom the boys had met during one of the searches of the opera house.

He listened to Joe's account of what had happened at the theater and wrote down the description of the van.

"You can go on to the hospital, Joe," Corey said when the Hardy boy had finished. "I'll call this in to Chief Collig immediately."

They were just approaching the gates to the naval base when Manuel pointed and cried, "Look at those bodies!"

Two guards lay on the road. Joe leaped out of Manuel's car and raced to them. At first, he, like Manuel, believed they were dead, but then he saw them breathing. Joe thought that he detected the smell of some kind of gas, but couldn't be sure. He carried the servicemen off the road and under a tree.

"Go on to the hospital," he requested when he got back into the car. "I just hope we're not too late."

As they drove up to the entrance, a man tore out of the main doors. Manuel had to slam on his brakes to avoid hitting him. "It's Dr. Smith!" Joe cried and put his head out of the window. "What's going on, Doctor?"

The startled man glanced over his shoulder as he headed towards the doctors' parking area. "The president has been kidnapped! A lot of people inside have been gassed. Go help them while I chase the crooks!"

Manuel turned off the engine and he and Joe ran into the hospital. Fenton Hardy, Captain Svensen, Mr. Jones, and many others were emerging from the gassy corridor.

"Dad, are you all right?" Joe asked.

"No time to talk now," Fenton Hardy said, moving unsteadily to the reception desk. He picked up a phone and dialed. "Collig? Am I glad I caught you in! I can't explain now, but the president has been kidnapped. Yes, I said the president. Take my word for it. Anyway, he's been taken away in some sort of vehicle. No, I can't tell you who the kidnappers are. I can't give you a description of the vehicle. You see, we were gassed for—what's that you say? Could it be the same vehicle Joe described to Dan Corey?" He turned and looked at his son who was nodding. "That's it, Chief. It seems like he knows things I don't. You have an all-points alert watch already? Good! We'll start working from here."

When Mr. Hardy hung up, Joe related all that had happened to him and introduced Manuel.

"But where is Frank?" his father asked. "He must still be in the children's ward, I guess."

"No, he isn't," came a groggy voice. Chet had walked up, shaking his head to clear it. "I don't know where he is, but he's not there. He and I came out and saw Zandro and Happy Hortell pushing this gurney with a man on it."

139

"The president of the United States," Joe informed his friend.

Chet's jaw dropped. "The president? No kidding! Well, we charged them and all I remember is Hortell shooting some gas at me until I woke up a minute ago."

A nurse who was questioned managed to shed some light on Frank's disappearance. "I saw a young man running out the door after the kidnappers," she explained. "He was dark-haired, about nineteen years old."

Fenton Hardy nodded. "What happened then?"

The nurse shrugged and said, "I don't know. He went out, that's all."

A search of the parking lot failed to provide any clue.

"My guess is that he caught up with Zandro and Hortell and that they took him along," Fenton Hardy said gloomily. "They could be headed anywhere—going to a plane or a boat or switching vans."

"Oh, I bet I know where they're going," Joe said.

His father stared at him. "Where?"

"To the opera house!"

15 Zandro's Hideout

Mr. Hardy stared at his son in surprise. "Why do you say that?"

"It makes sense, Dad," Joe insisted. "Why would Zandro go to all the trouble of scaring people out of the opera house if he didn't plan to use it?"

"Oh, it's logical, all right," his father agreed a bit testily. "The problem is that many things in life don't fit into a neat pattern. Yet I'll go along with your theory."

He looked up at the sky, which was full of circling helicopters. "Chief Collig and the FBI still think the kidnappers are headed out of town, but I don't see how they could make it with helicopters up there, all roads blocked, and the Coast Guard and the navy blocking the shore."

"Anyway, the police are covering all those escape routes," Joe said. "I say we try the opera house."

His father agreed, and soon they were driving to Bayport in the boys' car. Right behind them were Manuel and Chet.

"What's been going on, Dad?" Joe questioned.

"I'm not sure yet. All I know is that the vice-president has requested the news media to hold the story of the kidnapping until the government obtains all the facts. And that's our job right now—finding out exactly what happened and why."

Zandro had anticipated the moves that the government might make. He had taken a little-used back street to the city, just in case the police had set up roadblocks. He knew in advance that getting out of town would be impossible. Exactly fourteen minutes after he had gassed the guards at the gate of the naval base, he drove the van into an alley at the rear of the opera house.

Satisfied with his success so far, he got out, walked to the back of the van, and opened the doors. Then his smile turned to an angry frown. The presence of an outsider, especially a Hardy, was the last thing he wanted!

Hortell gave his boss no chance to complain. "I couldn't help it," he said tersely. "He jumped in just as we were starting off. I knocked him out, but I

142

didn't want to throw him into the road since he may realize what we're up to and put the cops on our tail."

Zandro made a sour face. "Well, you couldn't help it, I suppose. At worst, it's only an annoyance and doesn't affect our plans in the slightest. Watch it, he's coming to."

Hortell unlocked the rear door of the theater, ran in, and returned in a moment with a rope. Frank was quickly tied and gagged.

"These Hardys have been more trouble than I expected," Zandro grumbled. "But at last we have them under control with Joe in the trunk and Frank in our hands. Now let's carry the president in."

They put their unconscious prisoner on a stretcher and transported him into the theater. By this time, Frank was awake. He could not free himself during his captor's absence, however; he had been unable to use the Houdini trick that Joe had employed since he had been only half-conscious at the time.

In a few minutes, Hortell returned. He untied Frank's legs and roughly yanked the youth to his feet. "Get inside," the kidnapper ordered, pushing Frank in front of him.

They went to Zandro's old dressing room, through the closet panel, and then up the stairs to the storeroom Jonathan Ridoux had mentioned.

143

The ceiling was a dome through which the bright sunlight streamed. There were three cots; the president slept peacefully on one. I wonder what he's going to say when he wakes up, Frank mused. The only other furniture in the room was a kitchen table with two chairs. In a corner, food cans were neatly stacked.

"Welcome, Frank, welcome!" Zandro sneered as the Hardy boy was shoved through the doorway. "I hope you approve of our humble residence as it will be your home for an indefinite period. Make yourself comfortable. Happy, would you please seat our guest?"

Frank felt himself propelled along, then turned, tripped, and pushed down into a sitting position, his back to the wall.

"Of course, I realize that you would prefer to be elsewhere," Zandro said, chuckling and rubbing his hands, "but you insisted on coming along. Then again, you may appreciate the great moment you are witnessing. This is the first time a president of the United States has ever been kidnapped!"

Joe and his father were nearing the opera house when Joe begged, "Tell me what happened so far, Dad!"

Mr. Hardy nodded. "I better start at the beginning. You'll recall that I was summoned to Washington. Well, I was met at the airport by Mr. Jones, whose real name, by the way, is Rocco Orazio. He's a high-level official in the Secret Service. Some other government people were with him, and we held a conference right there. The news they had for me was certainly shocking."

"What did they tell you?" Joe urged.

"The president had a tumor, possibly cancerous. He needed to be operated on immediately, and it was to be done secretly and away from the Washington area so the public wouldn't be alarmed unnecessarily."

Joe was silent for a moment, then said, "Something like that has never happened before, has it?"

"Yes, it has. Grover Cleveland had a secret operation performed on the presidential yacht. Anyway, the Bayport Naval Hospital was chosen as the facility. My job was to be the local security man, and I was to coordinate with the Secret Service and the navy. No one else was to be let in on it. Not even Chief Collig was notified.

"As you know, Mr. Orazio and the men in the black car came to our house. He also brought the chief surgeon, whom you know as Smith, but whose real name is—"

Just then the CB crackled. Fenton Hardy picked it up and talked to Chief Collig. "You have all exits from the city blocked? Good!"

"We haven't seen hide nor hair of them so far," said the police officer. "Not a clue. It looks as if those magicians have disappeared into thin air."

"No magicians are that good," the detective said grimly. "We're following up on Joe's hunch and going to the opera house. I'll keep in touch with you."

He switched off and continued his story. "All went well, except for the Peter Wilkinson incident. But his publisher agreed to hold the story until later. The president arrived last night and was whisked off to the naval base. Everything was ready."

"Unfortunately, so was Zandro," Joe said tersely.

Mr. Hardy nodded. "The president was wheeled into the operating room. He was sedated, so I doubt he was aware of what happened next. I was leaving the operating room when I heard a noise in the corridor. I saw two men in masks squirting gas at the marine guards who were taken completely by surprise."

"I'm sure they didn't expect two magicians to attack them," Joe put in.

"Of course not. Anyway, I half-turned to shout a warning. As I did, I was aware of a person behind me. I didn't get a chance to sound the alarm because I was hit on the head and went out like a light. When I woke, the gas was clearing, people were getting up from the operating floor, and the president was gone."

Joe shot a quick glance at his father. "You mean that—"

His father nodded. "The kidnappers had an accomplice inside the operating room. That's *exactly* what I mean!"

16 Kidnapped!

The president had been tossing and turning for a
half-hour. Occasionally, he muttered in his deliri-
um. At last, he fell quiet. After a minute of this
peaceful interlude, he opened his eyes.

"Where am I?" he asked. "Is the operation over?"
He examined his surroundings. "This doesn't look
like a hospital room."

Zandro roared with laughter that was on the edge
of hysteria. "How astute you are, sir. That's why I
voted for you. Indeed, it is not a hospital room. Is
the operation over, you ask? It depends on what
operation you are referring to. Yours has not even
started while ours—an operation of a *different*
sort—has just begun."

148

The president frowned. "Where am I?" he repeated.

"Another good question," Zandro observed. "Let me inform you that you now reside in a historic theater, the Bayport Opera House, which is undergoing restoration. It was here that John Barrymore—"

"If this is a joke, then it has gone far enough," the chief executive said in a furious tone. "I'm not going to stay here and—"

Zandro sobered immediately as his prisoner tried to rise. "But you are going to stay here, sir, until the ransom is paid. I do wish you would not try to get up. If you persist, we will have to tie you like that." Zandro indicated Frank with a nod. "This is no joke, I assure you. We are deadly earnest."

The president sank back, recognizing the threat in the other's words. "How did you get me out of the hospital?"

Zandro reverted to the exuberant side of his personality. "With gas. Gas and surprises. No one expected us. They fell like tenpins beneath our charge."

"So you killed them all?"

Zandro looked indignant. "Killed? No, not at all. Do we look like killers? What do you take us for?"

"I take you for petty thugs who have managed to

kidnap the president of the United States," the prisoner said calmly.

Frank was fascinated by this verbal duel. He had heard that the president was not one to panic, and that he had been a war hero, cool under the worst fire. The description proved to be true.

"I think you are more frightened than you would have me believe," the president added.

"Frightened? I, Zandro the Great, magician extraordinaire, am never frightened!"

"Oh, no? Then why do you keep this young man tied and gagged? You must be terrified of what he might do to you."

"Do not let appearances deceive you," Zandro remarked. "This youth has the strength of ten. Yet you have a point. Happy, remove the gag."

Happy obeyed, but with obvious disapproval. Frank took a long, deep breath of fresh air.

"Who are you, young man?" the president asked.

"Frank Hardy, sir."

"Hardy, eh? I believe I have met your father, Fenton?"

"That's right."

"A good man. Well, Frank, you and I are in a hot spot, but, don't worry, we'll get out of it."

"Certainly, you will be out of it," Zandro said, "as soon as the government pays the ransom."

"And what will this ransom be?" the president asked.

"A billion dollars!" Zandro said with a smile.

"Fenton, we've had word from the kidnappers," Chief Collig said over the car radio. "They phoned the local TV station."

"They?"

"Well, one person, really. A man."

"What did he say?"

"That they wanted a ransom of one billion dollars!"

Fenton whistled. "They shoot high, don't they? They'll never get it, of course."

"Don't be so sure of it, Fenton. I believe the federal government will kick in with it."

"It's *after* the delivery I'm thinking of," Fenton said. "As soon as it's made, the FBI will close in like a steel trap."

"They've thought of that, too. It's to be sent to a Swiss bank."

This time, Joe whistled.

"Very clever," Fenton said. "They know how the Swiss feel about revealing the names of their customers."

"The caller said they want the payment within five days," Chief Collig went on. The TV station has agreed to keep mum on all this until authorized to pass it along to the public."

"Five days, eh?" Fenton said. "Let's hope we catch them long before that."

151

"It might not be easy," Chief Collig said glumly, indicating that he thought their chances were remote.

"A billion dollars!" The president looked at Zandro with amusement. "You haven't a chance of getting that amount."

"Oh, I think we will," the magician said, rubbing his hands in anticipation. "You underestimate your value." A dreamy look crept into his eyes. "Three hundred and thirty-four million dollars will make me one of the richest men in the world."

"All right, let's suppose that you do get this money. You'll never get it out of the country. You'll never get *yourselves* out of the country," the president warned.

"We've thought all that out, Mr. President. The money goes into our account in a Swiss bank. And, of course, we would receive guarantees of safe passage from the United States before we released you."

"But what country would accept you?" Frank broke in.

Zandro looked at him distastefully. "How naive you are, young Hardy. You would be surprised how many nations would be willing to accept us and our money." He chuckled. "You know, seeing how our plan is working out even to the smallest detail after

152

months of planning is a great satisfaction. But a greater satisfaction is knowing that we have completely outwitted the Hardys. Your father is lying unconscious in the hospital, you are here with your arms and legs tied, and your brother is in a trunk in the Palace Theater."

"In a trunk!" Frank cried. "He could die in there!"

"Perhaps," Zandro said smugly. "Perhaps he will have the famous Hardy luck and escape. He is no longer a problem. You see how my scheme is working out?"

Frank was scornful. "Your scheme? Who do you think you are fooling? It wasn't all your plan. In fact, I suspect it wasn't your idea at all."

Zandro's face was red with fury. "What do you mean? It was my idea, I tell you, mine!"

"Is that so?" Frank's voice was tinged with contempt. "You had to learn about the president's illness and the decision of having the operation take place at the Bayport Naval Hospital. You couldn't have guessed that. Then you had to know the exact moment the president was going into the operating room. Someone tipped you off about that. And how are you going to let the government know about the ransom? There's no phone in here. Lastly, you admitted you had a partner or partners without knowing you did."

"You lie!" the magician screamed. "I didn't."

"Yes, you did. A billion split two ways is five-hundred-million. Yet a few minutes ago, you said your share of the ransom would be three-hundred-and-thirty-four million dollars, or about one-third of the total. Therefore, a third person is involved in this."

The president looked at Frank with admiration. "A brilliant analysis. It escaped me altogether."

Furiously, Zandro advanced on Frank, his hands raised. "The entire thing was my idea—my idea, my planning, my leadership!"

Frank sniffed. "Manuel was right. You are nothing but a fat egomaniac!"

"Manuel!" the kidnapper shrieked and Frank realized too late that he had touched the most vulnerable spot in Zandro's armor. The upraised hands came down and his fingers spread like an eagle's talons until they squeezed Frank's throat. The youth looked up into the man's face, the eyes blazing with an insane light.

The image of Zandro began to fade as the pressure increased, and Frank felt himself slipping away into unconsciousness.

17   The Ransom

Chief Collig's voice came in on the radio again. "Fenton, a patrol car is waiting on Ocean and Seventh. When you come by, it will follow your car to the opera house. It's not that I don't believe in Joe's idea, but there's no use in taking chances."

"We're proceeding up Ocean now," Fenton replied. "I see the patrol car. We're passing it and it's swinging in behind us."

"Good. Check with me if anything comes up. Over and out."

"So Zandro and Hortell were the ghosts that Ridoux saw," the detective said after the police officer clicked off.

"They must have," Joe concluded. "Zandro told

me at the Palace that he had been behind the entire ghost legend. Of course, that had been the secret I fell across by accident."

Fenton Hardy turned and drove down an alley to the back of the theater, followed by Manuel's car. The police car stopped in front of the building, and one officer got out to take a position at the entrance. Then the car went down the alley.

Suddenly, Zandro's grip lessened and then relaxed completely. Dimly, Frank could hear Hortell exclaiming, "The cops are here. How did they find out so fast?"

Zandro's henchman was standing on a chair, peering out of a window in the dome.

"What are you talking about?" Zandro's insane fury had spent itself, and he stood up.

"I heard a siren, so I looked out. Three cars came down the alley. One was that yellow sports sedan the Hardys drive. The last one was a police car. It stopped and let out one cop. He's standing in front, Hortell related.

"Now don't get nervous, Happy," Zandro said. "They're probably just looking around. The entire city is being searched."

"That was quite an exhibition of bravery you put on a moment ago," the president said sarcastically, "trying to choke a young man who is bound hand

156

and foot. It must have taken a lot of courage." He looked over at Frank. "Are you all right, son?"

Frank nodded, although still gasping for breath. He realized that he had had a close call. He knew now that Zandro was not sane, but he hadn't thought the magician's mania would lead him to homicide.

"I admit that I have a quick temper," Zandro said calmly, "but he shouldn't have goaded me, especially about Manuel."

Fenton Hardy entered through the rear entrance first, followed closely by Officer Dan Corey and Joe. Bringing up the rear were Chet and Manuel.

Corey's large flashlight cast a beam over the orchestra seats. "I can go through the front and the basement," he said.

"They're not there," Joe said.

"Okay Son, you lead us," Fenton said gravely.

Joe motioned for everyone to go upstairs. At the top, he turned right and went down to room number 13. "Remember how Frank said he got through the closet by pulling a coat hook?" he asked and opened the closet door.

"But Zandro and Hortell wouldn't have taken the president down there," Chet protested. "The stairs are gone."

"There's an upper room, too," Joe said. His hand

touched the coat hook and the panel swung back. Fenton Hardy and his son stepped out onto the landing. The detective held up his hand as a signal to the others to maintain absolute silence. Then he and Joe started up the narrow stairway.

Suddenly, the door at the top was flung open. A smiling Zandro gazed down at them. "Good day, gentlemen," he said cheerfully. "So you found our little hideout, did you? We never planned that you would, especially so quickly. How did you do it? Is that Joe Hardy I see down there? Ah, that's the reason. You may not believe this, young man, but I am truly glad you escaped from the trunk. It occurred to me later that you might suffocate."

"No, I don't believe you," Joe said, gritting his teeth.

Zandro clucked, obviously enjoying himself. "Such skepticism. And the man in front of you must be the famous Fenton Hardy. I am most honored to meet you, sir. May I congratulate you on raising two fine sons. I would like to make one suggestion before we continue this conversation, though. Please stop coming up. In fact, it would be better for you to return to the bottom of the stairs, a much safer place for negotiations."

"What makes you think we will negotiate?" Fenton Hardy asked.

"Well, for one thing, we have your other son, Frank." There was a smug expression on Zandro's face. "If that fails to impress you, I might add that the president is also our guest." There was a touch of menace in his voice as he added, "I would hate seeing anything unfortunate happen to them."

Fenton Hardy nodded. "All right," he said. Then he and Joe retreated to the bottom of the stairs. "Notify Chief Collig that we've located the president and his kidnappers at the opera house," he whispered to Officer Corey who was standing in the closet.

"Yes, sir," Corey said and disappeared.

"It's little matter to us that you discovered our hideout," Zandro continued. "In a way, it is easier to talk. Not that there's much to negotiate. The billion dollars is transferred to a Swiss bank, our transportation to a foreign nation of our choice is guaranteed, and we release the president. Very simple."

"It may be simple to you," Fenton Hardy growled, "but not to anyone else. Anyway, I have no authority to make deals with you. You'll have to talk to government officials."

"Well, where are they?" Zandro cried petulantly. "Go get them."

"They have been sent for. Be patient."

The magician's scowling face broke into a smile. "I will indeed. After all, I have been so patient for so many weeks, planning this entire operation. I won't mind waiting a little longer."

Within ten minutes, a number of officials converged on the opera house. Four police cars and twenty officers blocked the front of the theater.

"It looks like an army," Happy Hortell said nervously.

Zandro shrugged. "So what? They are helpless. Cheer up, my friend. We'll soon be flying over the Atlantic, counting our money."

The president shook his head. "It's all folly, Zandro, as much of an illusion as any you present on stage. I urge you to surrender. The sooner you do that, the better it will be for you."

The magician flashed him a grin. "You are persuasive, Mr. President, as befits your high office, but not persuasive enough. No, this is the greatest trick that I have ever performed and it will work."

Since Zandro's attack, Frank had been ignored by the kidnappers. He struggled to free himself, but the ropes were tightly knotted.

Dan Corey led Chief Collig, Mr. Orazio of the Secret Service, and a mixed group of Bayport police and government men up to the dressing room. Fenton Hardy and Joe left the landing and stepped in to talk to them.

"Hello, Rocco," Mr. Hardy said. "Well, they've been found."

"Good work, Fenton." Orazio clapped the detective on the back.

"Don't congratulate *me*, Rocco. It was my son Joe who led us to the opera house."

"Our thanks to you, Joe. Now I'll talk to this Zandro."

When the Secret Service agent had identified himself, Zandro exclaimed, "Good! Now we're getting somewhere. You ought to have both the money and plane ready before nightfall."

"Nightfall? You're kidding yourself. In the first place, I can neither agree to nor refuse your demands. The vice-president has to be informed and only the Congress has the power to grant money. So you see—"

"I took civics in high school, too," Zandro snapped, "so don't lecture me as you would a child. All you have to do to notify the vice-president is to pick up a phone and call. Congress is still in session and, although it's Sunday, I imagine its members can be rounded up pretty fast when there is a national emergency—and, believe me, sir, this is a national emergency. So please spare me any further words and get on with your duty."

Orazio came back into the dressing room. "He doesn't know that the vice-president and Congress have known about the kidnapping for an hour. They are just waiting for word from us as to what they should do."

"What are you planning?" Fenton Hardy asked.

"I don't know," said the Secret Service agent in a tone of desperation. "I hate to see those gangsters up there get away with this, but so far I can't figure out how to get at them."

"For Pete's sake, Orazio, tell Congress to give them the money and a plane and let them go," a new voice pleaded. The doctor known to Joe only as Smith had arrived.

"Where did you come from?" Orazio asked. "We lost track of you after the kidnapping."

"I was trying to find the president," the doctor said, "but let's not go into that now. Don't you understand that a man's life may be at stake? The president is very, very ill. I've told you time and time again this operation cannot be delayed."

"There's a lot of truth in what he says, Rocco," Fenton Hardy said quietly.

Joe hurried from the room. Manuel caught up to him on the balcony. "Joe, where are you going?"

"I have an idea I'd like to try."

"And I have an idea, too. You tell me yours and I'll tell you mine. Maybe we could combine forces. We've got to rescue the president!"

18   A Clever Trick

Five minutes later, Joe and Manuel were in front of
the theater, explaining their ideas to Dan Corey,
who was in charge of the police at the entrance.

"It sounds like a thin chance to me," the veteran
police officer commented, "but who knows? It
might work with a little luck, and we sure need
some luck at the moment." He looked at Manuel.
"I'll assign a patrolman to drive you to the Palace
Theater. In the meantime, I'll give young Hardy a
boost."

In a moment, Manuel disappeared in a police car.
Corey looked up at the building. "Are you sure you
can handle this, Joe?" he asked dubiously. "That
roof seems kind of rickety."

Joe grinned. "Well, it won't be the easiest climb I've ever tried, but my brother and I have had plenty of experience going up cliffs a lot worse than this."

"Yes," Corey said, "but then you had plenty of equipment, right?"

"Right, but I don't have time now to go home and get the ropes, boots, crampons, axes—all that stuff."

"I guess you're right," Corey said. "I wouldn't let you do it, though, if we weren't in such a crisis. Okay, kid, up you go."

He joined his hands, forming a step. Joe put his foot into it and was hoisted up to the first window. Now he was on his own. His groping fingers searched for holds. Straining with all his strength, he slowly pulled himself up, his rubber-soled shoes aiding him.

There were no windows above the third floor, and there were still twenty feet to scale before he would get to the comparative safety of the domed roof. Near him, though, was a drain spout. He grabbed it with his left hand and tested it. It seemed sturdy enough. He then put his right hand on the old metal tubing and shimmied up. When he was within four feet of the edge of the roof, the rusty pipe gave way and Joe felt himself swinging into space. He caught a glimpse of Corey's shocked face down below.

At the last moment, though, he reached out to seize a metal strip that had supported the drain spout. The sharp, thin piece cut into the palm of his hand. He felt like screaming, but gritted his teeth; a loud cry might be heard by the people inside!

Fortunately, the metal strip held. He swung on it until he could whip his legs upwards. They caught on the edge of the gutter. Then he put his right hand on the gutter and released his hold on the metal strip.

He was afraid the old gutter might fall, too, after the drain pipe. To his relief, however, he discovered that it was made of wood. Although it was old and rotted in places, it was still strong enough to hold his weight.

Finally, he reached the roof and sat on it, his feet on the wooden gutter. He wrapped his wounded left hand with a handkerchief and waved to Corey who grinned, shook his head, and mopped his brow.

Then Joe saw a patrol car stop at the curb. Manuel got out. The small magician was dressed as though he was about to step upon the stage in his top hat, cape, and tuxedo. He carried a wand in one hand and a black medical-type satchel in the other.

He followed Corey's gaze upward and waved at Joe. "Happy landing!" he called. The Hardy boy did not dare to call back, but he raised his thumb in a good-luck gesture.

Just as Manuel disappeared inside, the nails holding the gutter ripped out. Once more, Joe felt himself slipping. He twisted and landed face down on the roof, groping desperately for a hold. The tiles were made of slate. They were still wet and slippery after an early morning shower. However, some had fallen off through the years, leaving gaps, and Joe was able to stop his descent by grabbing the exposed wood beneath.

Once more, he gave a sigh of relief. He glanced down four stories to the pavement and saw Corey's horrified expression. That would have been some drop, Joe thought. It wasn't the kind of happy landing Manuel had in mind for me.

Slowly and cautiously, he made his way to the curve of the domed roof. At last, his fingers grasped the bottom of the skylight. He inched ahead until his eyes were over the sill and he could see into the room.

Chet observed Manuel with a critical eye when the magician came into the crowded dressing room. "What are you going to do in that get-up?" the youth asked. "And where is Joe?"

"Joe and I are going to rescue the president," Manuel announced gravely. He moved slowly through the mob of police, FBI agents, and Secret Service personnel until he came up against Chief Collig.

"Where do you think you're going?" the head of Bayport's police force growled.

"Joe and I have developed a scheme to free the president!"

The chief gaped at him. "Are you crazy? What do you think the rest of us are doing? Somebody get him out of here!"

Suddenly, Rocco Orazio came into the room from the landing. He stared at Manuel. "Who is this guy?" he demanded.

"He's Manuel the Magnificent, a magician," Chet explained.

"He's also out of his mind," Collig said. "He says he's going to rescue the president."

"Listen to me," Manuel pleaded. "Joe and I thought up this plan. Right now, he's up on the roof—"

Fenton Hardy stuck his head out from the landing. "What did you say? What was that about Joe?" he interrupted.

"He's up on the roof, going towards the window where they're holding the president," the magician explained.

Mr. Hardy shook his head disapprovingly. "Why didn't the two of you tell me about it?"

"You were talking to that madman Zandro. We felt that we didn't have any time to lose. Now will you please listen to me?" Manuel asked.

"I guess we'd better, so that when your son does something stupid, Fenton, we'll be vaguely aware of what is happening," Orazio said bitterly.

Fenton Hardy's cheeks burned in a sudden show of anger. "If Joe came up with a plan, I'm sure it's a good one. Go ahead, Manuel."

When the magician had finished, Orazio whistled. "It's a wild scheme, all right, but it's so far out that it just might work."

Dr. Smith thrust himself forward. "It's insane!" he thundered. "You're dealing with a man's life and that man is the president of the United States. You've got to stop this!"

"You're in charge of everything that happens in the operating room, Doc," Orazio said, "and I'm in charge of rescuing the president. Anything that goes on in here is *my* responsibility."

"And quite a mess you are making of it," the doctor snapped. "I protest this plan of a stage magician and a teenage boy most vigorously."

"That's your prerogative," the Secret Service man said, "and I'm sure that I'm going to hear all about it when we get back to Washington. Until then, though, please stay out of my way." He stepped aside. "Go ahead, Manuel. The stage is yours."

Joe looked into the window of the dome, and wondered what was going on in the dressing room.

Manuel should have created the diversion by this time. If it wasn't soon, Zandro or Hortell might spot him. He saw Zandro standing in the doorway on the other side of the room, his back to the youth. Hortell stood a few steps behind the magician, also turned away.

The shadow of Joe's head fell on Frank and he looked up. For an instant, his eyes opened with surprise and joy. Then he immediately lowered his head so that the kidnappers would not follow his gaze to the window.

He did, however, stare at the president and clear his throat to get the chief executive's attention. Then he jerked his head upwards almost imperceptibly. The president glanced at the window, noticed Joe, then winked at Frank and smiled.

Manuel appeared on the landing. "Zandro, I am Manuel the Magnificent!" he shouted.

"I know who you are," Zandro growled and then yelled, "Where are the government representatives? What is going on?"

"They are conferring about collecting the ransom," Manuel answered gravely. "Until they get word from Washington, there is little they can do."

Zandro shrugged. "I understand. But why are you here?"

"You faked an accident last night and the show at

170

the Palace was cancelled. I realize that you did this in part to prepare for the kidnapping. But I believe there was a greater reason, Zandro. I think that you did not wish to face me on the stage. You did not want me to expose you for the second-rate amateur you are."

The kidnapper glared down the narrow stairway. "I did not wish to face you? Little man, you should be honored to even appear in the same theater as me."

Manuel went on as if his rival had not spoken. "While we have this little interlude, I asked the authorities in the next room to allow me to challenge you to the contest you have evaded so long. They have agreed."

"You're crazy!" Zandro hissed. "I do not have my equipment here. You know that."

"You most feared my special trick," Manuel continued, seemingly oblivious to the other's words, "the trick that has taken me so many years to make perfect. That terrified you, so you arranged for the sandbag to fall on the stage. Not that I blame you, but we ought to have the contest right now, you and I, in private, where no one can see you humiliated and where your embarrassment will be concealed."

"Humiliated? Embarrassment? Never!" Zandro screamed. "What trick are you talking about? I never heard of your special new trick!"

Manuel looked up at him with wide innocent eyes. "I thought everyone in the magic world had heard of it. My trick of becoming invisible before your very eyes."

"Charlatan!" Zandro sneered. "You and I know it can't be done."

"Ah, but I have done it!" Manuel returned.

"Bah! I challenge you, fool! Do it! Do it in front of me right now! Make yourself invisible."

Manuel smiled. "That is what I intend to do."

"Hey, Zandro, do you really think you should let him do that?" came the nervous voice of Happy Hortell.

"Shut up," Zandro replied. "All right, Manuel, make yourself invisible!"

"Very well. Observe closely." Manuel began to gesture with his hands while murmuring an incantation.

"Save me the hocus-pocus," Zandro said with contempt. "We all know about that. Do the trick if you can."

"I will now make myself invisible," Manuel said.

There was a sudden puff of smoke rising between the two antagonists.

"That's nothing but magician's smoke," Zandro howled. "You didn't think that was a trick, did you?"

"But you can't see me, can you?" Manuel's voice came out of the smoke. "So I'm invisible."

Another puff of smoke rose, nearer to the kidnapper. Zandro realized too late that he had been duped. He tried to close the door as Orazio and Mr. Hardy came out of the smoke and he didn't even hear the sound of broken glass behind him!

19 *The Third Accomplice*

The smoke at the door had been Joe's signal. When he saw it curling into the room and Zandro trying to shut the door, the youth hurled himself through the window. He rolled across the floor, leaped to his feet, and pinioned Zandro's arms.

During the conversation between Manuel and Zandro, Frank had pushed himself up the wall to a standing position. Despite being bound hand and foot, he knew he could be of help. Even before his brother reached the floor, Frank had launched himself at Hortell with a huge jump. They both fell. Hortell snarled as he got back to his feet. He was in the motion of kicking the helpless youth when he was stopped by a commanding voice.

"Don't do that! You're in enough trouble as it is already," Orazio ordered. The kidnapper slowly put his foot down. His hands hung at his side, his shoulders slumped, and his chin fell to his chest.

After Fenton Hardy had put handcuffs on Zandro, Joe leaned down to untie Frank. The older boy smiled. "I never thought you'd get here," he said. "What took you so long?"

In a few seconds, the room was swarming with people. "Let me through, let me through!" said Dr. Smith, shoving through the crowd. He shouldered Zandro aside as the magician cursed.

The doctor felt the president's pulse and then took his temperature. "We've got to get him to the hospital right away," he cried in alarm. "His condition is weaker. He must be transferred to the operating room without further delay."

"For once, we agree," Orazio said. "Okay, everybody clear a path. A stretcher is coming up."

As the president was being carried out, he ordered the attendants to stop by the Hardy boys. He shook hands with both of them. "Thanks, Frank and Joe. You certainly have a lot of courage."

Then he was gone, followed by the worried doctor. "I've got to go, too," Orazio said to Fenton Hardy. "I wish you would stay here and help Chief Collig interrogate the prisoners."

"I'd be glad to do it," Mr. Hardy said.

"Find out who the inside person is. I have a feeling that he's the real brains behind all this. While he's free, the president is not safe," warned Orazio.

"We'll do our best," Fenton Hardy promised and Chief Collig nodded his head vigorously.

"If you discover anything important, let me know. I'll be at the hospital." Orazio turned and started down the stairs. "Dr. Duvalier, wait for me. I'm going along, too."

"If you will excuse me," Manuel said faintly. "I think I will go to my hotel. This whole situation has taken a great deal out of me."

"Certainly, Manuel," Chief Collig said. "We're all grateful to you. You certainly played the part of 'Manuel the Magnificent'. Corey?"

"Yes, Chief," the veteran officer answered.

"Will you see to it that Manuel receives a ride to his hotel in a patrol car?"

"Right! Mr. Manuel, please step this way."

"Now, Fenton, suppose we do this," the chief said, when the heroic magician had gone. "I'll take Hortell down to the dressing room and question him there. You grill Zandro up here. Then you and I will get together and compare notes."

"Fine," the private detective agreed, "but I'd like to make one suggestion. Since both my sons and Chet know these crooks, why don't you take Joe and

Chet with you and I'll let Frank sit in when I question Zandro?"

Five minutes later, both criminals were informed of their rights. Then the interrogations began.

"We want to know who was in this plot with you," Fenton Hardy said.

Zandro, who was sitting on one of the chairs, shrugged. "You know that. Happy Hortell."

"Besides Happy Hortell."

"Your son questioned me on that point already," Zandro said in an annoyed tone, indicating Frank with a jerk of his head. "I told him then, and I will tell you now, only Happy and I planned and executed the kidnapping."

Fenton shook his head. "That won't do and you know it. There are too many gaps, too many unanswered questions. For example, how did you know the president was going to be operated on in Bayport? When you found that out, you burned down the Boston theater, didn't you, and arranged for the transfer of the magician tournament?"

Zandro smiled. "It was a brilliant touch, wasn't it, burning down the theater?" Then his face darkened. "Only that fool, Manuel, managed to guess it."

"All right, you've answered one of the questions I asked," the detective noted. "Now how about telling me how you knew the president was going to be operated on at the Bayport Naval Base Hospital?"

Zandro assumed an arrogant expression. "I'm psychic, didn't you know? Frank here can verify it."

Fenton Hardy looked at his son, who smiled and shook his head.

"You still insist you were in this alone?"

"Happy Hortell—"

"With the assistance of Happy Hortell and no one else?"

The magician leaned back. "That is correct."

"Then who tipped you off as to the precise moment the operation was to take place? That wasn't decided until the very last second. You couldn't have known that when you went to the hospital."

No answer.

"Who hit me in the operating room?"

Zandro maintained his silence.

"Who called the TV station and gave the ransom terms?"

"I planned everything," Zandro said, looking bored. "Now if you are quite done with me, please conduct me to the local jail."

"You know, Zandro, that you are in a very difficult position. You may be imprisoned for the rest of your life," Fenton Hardy said sternly. "However, some leniency might be recommended in exchange for your cooperation. This is only a bit of

178

advice; I am not actually authorized to make such an offer, but after my long years of experience in these matters, I can categorically say—"

"Mr. Hardy, my elaborate plot has failed," Zandro interrupted. "My life lies in ruins. I need no crystal ball to tell me that my future years will be spent behind bars. To you, I suppose, I possess no virtue. But you are wrong. I do have one virtue to which I have always clung . . . and that is loyalty. I will hold to that principle even though to violate it would perhaps mean my release."

"You won't reveal who the third conspirator is?" Fenton Hardy asked.

The magician flashed a wry smile, but said nothing.

"We'll take a short break," the detective told the five police officers and two Secret Service men in the room. "Keep an eye on him. Come on, Frank."

Father and son went down the stairs to the dressing room. They arrived just in time to hear Happy Hortell say, "I'll say it again. I didn't know of any other guy in the plot. Yeah, sometimes I kind of suspected there was someone else—how could Zandro get all that inside information, I figured— but that was his business and not mine. Why should I care who got the third share? Over three-hundred-million bucks with no taxes was good enough for me."

"You don't have a clue then?" Chief Collig asked. "Not even a guess?"

Hortell shook his head unhappily. "Believe me, Chief, if I did, I'd be spilling it right here. Anything for a break."

The police chief motioned Fenton Hardy, Frank, Chet, and Joe out into the hall. "I think he is telling the truth," Collig said in a low voice.

"So we're stymied," the detective observed. "We could grill Zandro for days and I don't think he'd crack. He's not the average kind of criminal. I feel that he looked upon this whole thing more as an adventure—a way of tempting fate—than as a money-making scheme. After all, he is a very successful performer."

"If there was only a way of figuring it out," Collig mused aloud.

"Well, let's try," Fenton Hardy said. "Let's take one situation in which we know the third person was involved. What tipped Zandro off at the children's show that the operation was about to take place, that the president was being wheeled into the operating room?"

Chet raised his hands in a gesture of helplessness. "I didn't see any signal. The only thing that happened was when that doctor—"

"—came into the ward," Frank jumped in, excited.

"What doctor?" Fenton Hardy asked sharply.

"Smith! The one who was here, who went off with the president, who stayed in our house!"

"Dr. Duvalier!"

Something clicked in Joe's mind. He could now vividly remember sitting in a chair after Manuel had rescued him at the Palace Theater. He had looked at the trunk that could have been his coffin. On it were the words:

RUDOLPH DUVALIER
ZANDRO

"Duvalier is Zandro's last name!" Joe cried. He snapped his fingers in anger. "I should have remembered that when I heard Mr. Orazio call Smith Dr. Duvalier!"

"Are you sure?" his father exclaimed.

"Pretty sure," Joe said. "I saw it printed on the side of Zandro's trunk."

Fenton Hardy tore back into the dressing room and up the stairs, followed by Collig, Chet, and his sons. He stopped in front of Zandro and pointed a finger at him. "Your name is Duvalier, isn't it? Dr. Claude Duvalier is your brother, right?"

The magician turned pale. He said nothing, but his face was admission enough.

Mr. Hardy turned to the others. "Duvalier is going to operate on the president! We've got to notify Orazio immediately!"

181

20 Dangerous Operation

"Duvalier?" Orazio replied at the other end of the line. "That's hard to swallow."

"Believe me, it's true, Rocco," Fenton Hardy insisted. "You've got to postpone the operation, call in another surgeon, arrest—"

"Too late," the Secret Service man groaned. "He's already operating."

"Maybe you can get another doctor to take over at this point."

"I'll try," Orazio said grimly and hung up.

The detective came out of the phone booth. "The operation has already begun," he announced gloomily.

"Think of that man holding a knife on the president," Chief Collig said. "Let's go out there!"

Fenton Hardy, the chief, and the three youths traveled to the Bayport Naval Hospital in two police cars. They hurried up to the observation gallery overlooking the operating theater. Rocco Orazio motioned them to sit in his area.

"We tried to substitute another surgeon," he informed them, "but were told by several physicians that it would be disastrous at this point. We simply can't stop Duvalier now. All we can do is hope for the best."

Time passed slowly. Seconds seemed like minutes, minutes like hours. The Hardys looked on in fascination at the people dressed in green moving silently around the table on which the unconscious chief executive lay. The man in the center—Claude Duvalier—held the president's life in his hands. One slip of a surgical knife—accidental or deliberate—would kill the patient!

The doctor looked up at them once, his icy blue eyes mocking their helplessness. Then he continued with his work. Finally, he nodded at his nurse and stepped back. Then he turned and hurried out. Rocco Orazio was on his feet and moving in a flash.

There were three government men at the door to the operating theater. "Duvalier hasn't stuck his head out yet," one of them said when he saw his boss.

"Not yet?" Collig looked at Orazio. "That sounds bad."

"I don't know," the Secret Service man said. "This is the only exit. My guess is that he's taking off his gown and washing up."

One of the men standing by the door looked in the round window. "Here he comes!"

"Everyone back!" Orazio ordered. A wide circle was formed around the entrance.

Out came Claude Duvalier accompanied by another doctor. "I think the crisis is over, but the next few hours will tell," Duvalier said.

"A brilliant operation," his colleague commented. "You were magnificent!"

Duvalier laughed. "I appreciate the words, but they are somewhat exaggerated."

"All right, hold it right there," Orazio ordered.

Duvalier looked around at the group of tense men. "Won't you please allow Dr. Tremont to pass?" he asked calmly. "As you know, he had nothing to do with the kidnapping."

Orazio nodded. "Go ahead, Dr. Tremont."

Tremont cast a frightened look around and hurried down the corridor. Duvalier studied Orazio with an amused air. "I'm not trying to escape, Rocco. I'm not that foolish. As soon as I saw the Hardy boys in the gallery, I knew my little secret had been discovered. So I accept the inevitable."

"Little secret!" Orazio exploded. "I don't call a billion dollars little."

"It is a lot of money," Duvalier admitted. "How did you find out that I was involved in this scheme? Was it my brother who told you?" He shook his head. "I never thought he would."

"We did find out through him, but not from him," Fenton Hardy said. "He just happened to have the family name on his theatrical trunk."

"Ah, such a little thing." The surgeon sighed. "But the entire plot that Zandro and I devised so brilliantly was foiled by a number of little things. Remember that old children's tale that begins, 'For need of a nail, a kingdom was lost?' Something about a king or general losing an important battle because his horse's shoe came off. It seems that is still true."

"We were afraid that you would kill the president in revenge," Chet blurted.

Duvalier drew himself up proudly and pinned Chet with a haughty gaze. "Young man, it's true that I attempted the greatest kidnapping in history," he said coldly, "but I am not a murderer. I am a doctor first and foremost. My job is to preserve life, not destroy it!"

Two weeks later, a small party was held in the president's hospital room. The guests were Rocco Orazio, Fenton Hardy, Frank and Joe, Chief Collig, Chet, Manuel, Mrs. Hardy, and Aunt Gertrude.

The First Lady was seated by her husband's bed when they entered, but she rose to greet them. "I don't know how to thank you all. We both owe you a great debt. As you know, I had to stay in Washington so as not to make the media suspicious. I spent the day in agony after I heard that my husband had been kidnapped. My only hope was in the fact that I knew the Secret Service, the police, and Mr. Hardy were on the job."

"Marge, you forgot those young men," the president said with a smile and waved at Frank, Joe, and Chet. "One of them jumped through a window and another knocked down a kidnapper. When I think about them, I have no worries about the younger generation."

He looked beyond the Hardys to the small man standing bashfully in the rear. "There's also the magician who risked his life to confront those gangsters with his gift of gab and a couple of smoke bombs."

"It was nothing," Manuel said modestly.

"Maybe to you it was nothing," the president said, "but it meant a lot to us. To show our thanks, we would like you to give a show at the White House."

Manuel's face lit up with joy. He knew he could never buy the publicity that a command performance at the White House would bring him.

"You look very well, Mr. President," Orazio said.

"Flatterer!" the president grinned. "And a liar, too. What you mean is that I look a lot better than when I arrived. I admit I feel a lot better, too. You know, every doctor who has examined me has raved about the operation. A masterpiece, they call it. It seems a shame that someone like Claude Duvalier would throw his life away on a stupid scheme. It's strange the way some people's minds work. How is everything proceeding with those men, Rocco?"

"Nothing much at the moment," Orazio said. "There probably will be a trial in the fall at the earliest. As you know, all three have confessed." He chuckled. "The only variance in the three statements is that Zandro insists he and only he thought up the whole thing."

"What an ego!" Joe said.

"You know, I'm inclined to believe some of his contention," his father stated. "The plot had a lot of the magician's art about it."

"How do you figure that, Mr. Hardy?" the First Lady asked.

"There were so many illusions, and illusions are what magicians depend on: the illusion of a ghost, the illusion of a benevolent Zandro. Also, Zandro was always diverting our attention as magicians do; they prepare the trick with their right hand while they make us rivet our eyes on their left hand."

"How did Zandro do that?"

"His real goal was to get into the hospital and kidnap your husband, but we could never guess that since he initiated a series of fake crimes, mainly against himself, in order to cast suspicion on Manuel. You see, we were looking at Manuel rather than him. He made a ghost out of Jonathan Ridoux to disguise his real intent concerning the opera house, namely, to make sure it was deserted when the president was kidnapped. It might have worked, too, if Frank hadn't found that poor old man."

"What's going to happen to Ridoux?" the president asked. "I hope he won't get sent to jail."

"The judge gave him one year in prison and then suspended the sentence," Chief Collig contributed. "In addition, the Bayport Community Arts Association has designated him as the official guide of the restored opera house."

"They couldn't have made a better choice," Frank said. "He knows plenty about it."

Suddenly, the young detective realized that he and his brother would be out of a job—and they weren't really happy unless they had a mystery to solve! His fears were unfounded, however, because a new case was already taking shape, called *Tic-Tac-Terror*.

Just then, two nurses' aides entered, carrying trays of ice cream, soft drinks, and cake. "Well, that's enough of what happened," the First Lady said. "Now to more important things—like eating!"

The president groaned. "What a thing to do to a wounded man—eat in front of him! You know that I'm only allowed to have soup."

"You'll be on solids next week," his wife said unsympathetically. "Anyway, you have to lose some more weight."

The patient smiled. "You're right. Also, it's a pleasure to see real food for a change, even though I can't have any."

When they had finished, Manuel stood. "Watch this," he said. He reached out his hand and plucked a medal out of the air. His audience applauded. "I believe this belongs to the Hardy brothers," he exclaimed and passed them the medal.

Frank read the inscription. "'To the two greatest magicians in the world.' Thanks, but how do you figure we deserve this?"

"Because you performed three of the greatest tricks I have ever seen."

"Which are?" Joe inquired.

"First, you made a ghost come to life. Second, you found a president where there wasn't supposed to be any."

"And third?"

"The third was the greatest trick of all. You made my troubles disappear overnight!"

You are invited to join

THE OFFICIAL NANCY DREW ®/
HARDY BOYS ® FAN CLUB!

Be the first in your neighborhood to find out about the newest adventures of Nancy, Frank, and Joe in the **Nancy Drew** ®/ **Hardy Boys** ® **Mystery Reporter,** and to receive your official membership card. Just send your name, age, address, and zip code on a postcard *only* to:

The Official Nancy Drew ®/
Hardy Boys ® **Fan Club**
Wanderer Books
Simon & Schuster Building
1230 Avenue of the Americas
New York, New York 10020

OFFER VALID ONLY IN THE UNITED STATES.